I0689804

Death on the Vine

A taste of wine, roses, money — and murder

L. Lee Kane

TSL Publications

First published in Great Britain in 2022
By TSL Publications, Rickmansworth

Copyright © 2018, 2022 L. Lee Kane

ISBN: 978-1-915660-26-8

The right of L. Lee Kane to be identified as the author of this work has been asserted by the author in accordance with the UK Copyright, Designs and Patents Act 1988.

All characters and events in this publication, other than those clearly in the public domain, are fictitious and any resemblance to actual persons, living or dead, is purely coincidental.

All rights reserved. No part of this publication may be reproduced, stored in a retrieval system or transmitted, in any form or by any means without the prior written permission of the publisher, nor be otherwise circulated in any form of binding or cover other than that in which it is published and without a similar condition being imposed on the subsequent buyer.

Cover by: Krista Lynn Designs
www.kristallynn.com/designs

{ 1 }

"Penicillin cures, but wine makes people happy."
ALEXANDER FLEMING

I often remind myself of the moment when my normal life changed and became abnormal. When I was six years old, my mother became ill. She often locked herself in the bathroom for hours with the lights off and the shower running. The one time I knocked on the door is forever ingrained in my mind. She opened it just enough to peer through the crack. After yanking me into the bathroom by my arm, she held me in a bear hug and screamed.

That was the beginning of her sucking the youth from my life.

What once was just a whisper about my mom and her "sickness" became a loud voice that spread like wildfire amongst the town gossips. Mom never recovered. Nor did I. She stole my childhood and ran off with me to southern California. We left my dad, my dog, the daisy bushes we planted, and all my friends when we moved to the concrete jungle of Inglewood.

Every morning was the same — until the next indelible marks of trauma. Rising from my small twin bed in the corner of my room, I threw off my thin pink coverlet, put on my best thrift-store purchase of a worn-out tee shirt and shorts, then stepped into the old dark, dank hallway and made my way to the kitchen. I hadn't wanted to use a light to help me find my way because it only reminded me of what I didn't have anymore — life on a large farm with a father, family, and the closeness of a small community in the green hills and Yosemite Mountains as a backdrop.

Stepping out the front door into the alley wasn't any more delightful; garbage cans were always strewn with remnants of food and rat droppings. But this school of hard knocks gave me three valuable lessons in my formative years.

First, walking was only used when indoors; jogging was the preferred method for outside destinations. Living in Inglewood was like being a moving target so running between home and school was the best way to survive people with knives or guns. Lesson number two: treat all loud noises as a cue to "stop, drop, and, roll" behind the nearest object. And finally, when spotted by the locals, act as if I was being confronted by a bear, meaning play dead.

Given the quality of life that Inglewood offered, I promised myself I'd move out at the first opportunity.

{ 2 }

"Wine is the most civilized thing in the world."
ERNEST HEMINGWAY

High School, Senior Year

Engine off, lights off, and the car in neutral. We glided up to my mom's apartment and slid into a front parking space. The house lights were still on inside. I was late getting home from the football game and hoped to sneak in without being noticed. I grabbed my pom-poms from the back seat and held my breath as I made my way to my cage where I locked myself away to avoid the torture and abuse. I stopped to wave a silent goodbye to my friends.

"Bye, Daisy," they whispered in chorus as they waved back.

Cheerleaders. I shook my head, grimacing at the possibility of being caught past curfew.

I really didn't want to leave the safety and security of my friends. I didn't live in a home. I lived in Hell. Every day was a new threat to me. Mom's latest husband Mike was a monster, especially after he had a few too many beers. If I were late, like I was now, I'd pay in some form. This was the only time he became creative. Sometimes he beat me. Other times I was grounded to my bedroom for long hours and forced to make my bed over and over. Occasionally other awful things happened to me. My mother put up with the abuse because we had nowhere else to go, no money, no family, but I was the one who always paid.

I plastered my ear to the front door, hoping to hear silence on the other side. Inserting the key slowly into the lock, I turned the handle. Again I listened, trying to hear any reaction. I pushed the heavy door open ever so slightly and peeked into the apartment.

On this rare occasion, no one was in the front room so the pain in the pit of my stomach lessened somewhat. I tiptoed silently down the hallway toward the bedrooms. At my mother's bedroom door I caught sight of what looked like the ghostly aberration of her standing in front of her bed. My head shouted at me to move on and run to my bedroom while no one noticed me, but I couldn't budge. I had to look around the room.

A gun dangled from her hand.

I didn't see Mike so I pushed the door open wider. It creaked, but Mom didn't seem to notice. Apprehensively I walked toward her. In horror I saw what she was standing over.

"Oh, my God, Mom! Oh, my God! What have you done?" Mike's face looked like a bowl of cherry Jell-O. She'd done that to him. The bedroom and her nightgown were covered in blood.

Breathe, Daisy, deep breaths, I said to myself, fixating on the one spot in the room without blood. That was the picture frame with my mom and Mike at a nightclub — the worst day of my life or so I'd thought right until this very moment.

Every muscle in my body shook. My right eye twitched, and the only thing that kept me from falling apart was my arms wrapped around myself. I hoped this was only a dream.

Sadly, it wasn't.

When I opened my eyes, I looked down at Mike's body, and bile rose in my throat. Focus on something else, I thought, like the horrible picture on the nightstand.

Slowly the need to puke faded, but every nerve in my body was on edge.

Mom dropped the gun next to Mike, and it sounded like a freight train when it hit the floor. She walked out of the room like nothing was wrong. As for me, I wanted out of there. I didn't even think about jumping over the blood splatter on the floor and followed her into the kitchen.

She was filling the coffee pot with water. You're making coffee?" Unforking believable!

"What do you mean, Daisy? And don't speak to me like that. Do you want me to wash your mouth out with soap?" She leveled the coffeepot with cup in hand to pour me coffee, at me as if this was just some normal Saturday morning conversation. "Holy shit, Mom! Do you have any idea what you've done?"

She sat the coffeepot down and put a finger to her lips. "Sssh, Daisy, be quiet. Mike's asleep. He was drinking at the Torchlight Club with his friends and then decided to come home and scream at me. He even hit me."

"Mom, we need to get you into the shower, and then I'll call the police." Maybe not! They'd take one look at her, figure they had an open-and-shut case, and keep the paperwork to a minimum by tossing her in a funny farm and me in juvenile hall or foster care. My mom might not be my biggest protector, but I knew enough about the foster care system to know I didn't want to go into it. I'd never see her again. No matter her faults, she was still my mom.

I stopped and thought for a moment. Of all the times that I took a beating from Mike, not once did my mother step in to stop him or call the police, but one punch to the arm, and she pulls out a gun and shoots Mike in the head. I hated her, and I loved her. How screwed up was that?

{ 3 }

"Wine improves with age.
The older I get the better I like it."
ANONYMOUS

I walked out the back door and down toward a vacant lot at the rear of our apartment. Using my Girl Scout skills to light a fire, I tossed my mom's bloodied nightgown and towels into a pile and set them on fire. I waited until they became ash, smothered the embers, and buried the evidence. I ran back to our apartment and headed straight for Mom's bedroom. An old large sleeping bag was stuffed in the back of Mike's closet. I needed to put him into something so it might as well be that.

In our garage unit I unearthed my old red wagon. If it hadn't have been so late, I would surely have aroused the suspicion of every resident in the complex. I brought the cart to the apartment and folded Mike into the sleeping bag and dragged him into the cart. His blood now covered my new white cheerleading sweater. There was no time to worry about that now. I wheeled him out into the garage and began to salvage anything I could to help me. Looking over piles of our old things, I spotted a door we had replaced after Mike's fist put a hole in it one drunken night.

Beside it was a pristine punching bag. I dragged it to my truck and lifted it onto the tailgate. Then I tied an extension cord around Mike's body, and after tossing the loose end over one of the rafters, tied the other end to the punching bag. The weight and force of the punching bag was just enough to help me lift Mike out of the wagon. Slowly I pulled the truck forward until Mike's body was high enough off the ground that I could get him in the truck.

Somehow I managed to push the punching bag off the tailgate and swing Mike over the truck's bed. I cut the extension cord, the tension so tight it nearly whipped me in the face. One job down and umpteen to go.

{ 4 }

"Compromises are for relationships. Not wine."
SIR ROBERT SCOTT CAYWOOL

I was sweating, shaking, and my muscles ached. Either shock or adrenaline propelled me. It was time to check on Mom. She was still standing in the shower where I had left her. I took her out and told her to dry herself off while I got her some clothes to wear.

I guided her to the front room and draped a coat around her shoulders. We needed to take a drive.

Stopping at the red light just past Creek Park Shopping Center, the streets were empty except for me, my mom, and a dead Mike. My white-knuckled hands gripped the steering wheel as sweat dripped into my eyes. The only thing that kept me from puking out the window was my agitation from the constant noises emanating from my mother.

I prayed to God that the cops wouldn't stop us. How could I explain being out in the middle of the night, covered in dirt, blood, and ash with a shovel and a body in the back of my truck? I didn't think hunting for buried treasure in Inglewood would suffice. The light turned green, and I slowly took my foot off the pedal, looking both ways as I crept into the inter-section.

"Daisy, you'd look so much prettier if you cut your hair shorter and lost a few pounds."

"What?" I couldn't flippin' believe she was saying this to me after what she had just done.

My mother's husband for the year — I never asked her "What's new?" I asked her, "Who's new?" — was a violent, sloppy drunk who came home late Friday nights. Tonight he said that he was driving over to Creek Park Shopping Center off of Blackstone to meet up with some friends of his, probably some other drunken fools. Creek Park was the side of town where the wealthy people lived, and that's where I was headed.

I drove down to the ground floor of the shopping center's double-decker parking garage, which was partially under construction for repaving. Lucky for me I found a hole that was partly dug. I turned off the lights and stopped there. I pulled down the tailgate and rolled Mike out — right on top of me. His body slammed into mine so hard we both tumbled down into the hole. I struggled to get him off me, and a sense of claustrophobia overcame my senses. The panic worked, and I was free of him but not my shaky nerves. I retrieved a pick and shovel and went to work. I needed to dig at least an extra three feet of dirt to completely cover Mike. Hopefully when the construction workers poured the concrete, this problem would be solved.

"Daisy, it's three o'clock in the morning, and the stores are closed." I suddenly heard my mom's anxious voice. "What are we doing here?" I couldn't believe she didn't remember what she had done. Or did she?

"Shhh, Mom! I lost my watch; I think it's in this hole. I'll be there in a minute." I had to figure out a way to get the hole deeper. Mike was fat, and his literal dead weight was heavy. The hole was deeper than I thought and had simply filled up from the dragging backhoe bucket. I shoveled dirt out and then did my best to flatten the bag he was in. I quickly crab-walked up the side of the hole; I couldn't breathe. I began shoveling dirt from the edge and into the hole.

I pushed, shoved, and packed as much dirt on top of Mike as I could, hoping the construction workers wouldn't notice anything and just pour the asphalt right over him. This always seemed to work in the mob movies where hitmen made people disappear. "Daisy," my mother whined. "I'm tired; let's go now. What are you doing with that shovel?" Mom was watching me closely.

"Nothing, Mom. Everything's fine." Throughout my life, I'd learned a few things from her. The first was to use my motherly instincts to protect my kids, not an abusive husband. The second was to have an actual interest in somebody human when it came to choosing a husband rather than chasing money and a direct descendant of a baboon.

"Young lady, look at you; you're all covered in dirt, and you should be ashamed of yourself. When will you ever grow up?"

"I think tonight would be a good time, Mom. How about tonight?"

"Oh, okay, but I'm still going to have to go home and wash that sweater. What will the neighbors think of you?"

"I have no idea. Right now, I'm way too tired to care."

"Daisy, a security guard is coming this way; we shouldn't be here."

Geez, what else could go wrong?

He was talking into the walkie-talkie on his epaulet. The young security guard slowly approached, shining his flashlight on us. "Hello."

In my best friendly, sweet voice I said, "Hello. I'm so sorry. We had a flat tire so I pulled under the garage area where it was safer to change it."

"That was good thinking; you should always be cautious. Have you already finished changing your tire? Hey, it looks like you've ruined your sweater."

"Oh, no," I said, looking down. "My cheerleading sweater is all stained with dirt and grease." To add to the drama, I began to cry.

"Daisy, what's wrong? We need to get home; it's way past your bedtime."

"Can I help you? Are you hurt?"

Sniffling back more tears, I released the exhaustion I felt in every muscle of my body. "No, just exhausted, but thank you so much. I better get my mom home."

I hurriedly jumped into the driver's seat of my bloody truck and cautiously drove home.

The dirt began to move under the rubble, and a hand popped out, clawing its way out of the dirt pit.

Early the next morning I wearily rolled out of bed and called out to my mom. There was no answer. I had left her sleeping on the couch, but she wasn't there. My heart raced. Where was she? I ran to the garage in a panic.

The car was gone, and her suitcase that sat beside the water heater was missing. I never felt so alone or so isolated.

I picked up the house phone and called the police. "My mom," I said, "Bridgett Murphy, killed her husband."

{ 5 }

"Beer is made by men, wine by God!"
MARTIN LUTHER

Hans Weizner held up a hand-blown, dark-green glass capped with a stubby seal of thick black wax. It had no label, but etched into the glass in a spindly hand was the year 2000 and the words "Mission de Madonna Noire."

Evidence suggested that this wine belonged to a famous winery in France and that the bottle was considered to be one of the world's most significant rarities. The color was remarkably deep for its age and the value inestimable, at least to some people.

Hans thought he would store it in his private wine cellar in the basement of his home, along with the many oak barrels of expensive wine he and Andrew stole from a wealthy entrepreneur. The entrepreneur was a modern-day robber baron who made a profit off third world countries engulfed in chaos by taking what little valuables they had only to turn around and sell them to the highest bidder, men who cared little for how an antiquity or gem was attained. Hans found it funny to think that the rich guy hailed from a country such as Switzerland, a nation committed to neutrality. I guess he feels that as long as I'm not the one pulling the trigger, then I'm still neutral, he thought to himself.

In addition to collecting wealth from the poor, the Swiss gentleman collected barrels of wine and stored them in a vault-type cellar where only he could view the vast collection. Hans always thought that an item such as this rare bottle of wine was never meant to live forever but to be enjoyed for its richness.

One night he had some things to work out in Switzerland, and Hans put stealing this particular brand of wine as the aperitif for a long day of grueling tasks and errands. In the back of his mind, he was worried that the Swiss would come looking for him one day. At least it wouldn't be public because of his occupation in shady dealings.

Hans soon thought of his future — the money he would make and how Oakhurst, California would play a part in his game of cat and mouse. No one in this city would suspect him of anything except for being a wealthy European businessman bringing wine and culture to a small town. Well, he'd provide them that and so much more…

{ 6 }

"Drinking good wine with good food in good company is one of life's most difficult civilized pleasures."
MICHAEL BROADBENT

Immediately after high school graduation in 1990, I got a job in a winery hosting the tasting room, meeting new people, and learning everything I could about the intricacies of wine. It was an exciting experience that I learned a great deal from. After making enough money to attend college, I packed what little I owned, grabbed my diary, and jumped into my white 1984 two-door Toyota pick-up truck. It wouldn't have won any beauty contests, except maybe the truck that was least pleasing to the eye.

Inglewood, California was where my life took a sharp left turn. After Mom ran off, I was placed in a foster home until I turned eighteen. Since my birthday was in February, I was soon aged-out. The government didn't pay for foster kids who were on their own. "No money, no room" — so many nights I slept in my truck. If I was lucky, sometimes my friends let me stay at their homes. Most parents didn't want to have their kids spend the night with a kid whose mom had murdered her husband and her daughter put in juvenile hall for helping to cover it up. Maybe bad genes were inherited?

I needed out of the past and a new future. I decided to make the journey north for two reasons. First, it was anywhere but Inglewood, and second, I wanted to become a viticulturist, one who studies wine and wine making and hopefully at a school that wouldn't cost me my future wages fifty years after

I graduated. I was in the agricultural department throughout high school and found hope in creating life in plants. Maybe this was my salvation. I knew this was my only hope for a new life, away from what my mother had done.

I left Los Angles at two a.m. It was the only time there was little to no traffic. I drove up the Grapevine and stopped to eat at the In-N-Out Burger in Fraser Park. It was my last goodbye, and I celebrated with hamburger, fries, and a chocolate shake. Walking back to my truck, I had a feeling of fear of change, or maybe it was the guilt of leaving what was familiar. I was hopeful the feeling would pass with each mile I put between southern California and me.

Through the dried-up hills of the Tejon Pass, I descended toward Bakersfield through a golden valley in varying shades of amber.

As I drove down the giant hill, the sun was peeking out from behind the Tehachapi Mountains just east of Bakersfield where the land was a flatbed of soil as far as I could see. It would have been pleasant to stop and view my surroundings, but today wasn't one to stop.

Highway 99 was a four-lane highway divided by giant oleander bushes. On either side of the road were small rectangular signs identifying the different crops growing — oranges, pomegranates, grapes, apricots, almonds, plums, and pistachios.

During the Great Depression, the Dust Bowl of the Great Plains drove many workers to migrate to this region of California. Men and women made the exodus from Oklahoma and surrounding states hoping to find a new life for themselves and their families. I planned to do the same for myself.

In each field that I passed, Hispanic farm workers were sweltering in the blazing sun. They wore the same uniforms — baseball caps draped with a red or blue bandanna and long-sleeved shirts and jeans to protect themselves from the sun. They moved through the rows of vines, clipping off clusters of table grapes or picking oranges or plums and placing them in company-labeled bins. They, like the Midwest migrants, were searching for their American Dream.

Continuing my journey, I saw signs that read "Get Rid of Politicians." Other signs read "Jesus Is Lord," "Abortions Stop a Beating Heart," "No Water = No Jobs," and "High-Speed Rail Versus Food." It was all disconcerting.

Driving past the dairies in Hanford, the smell of dung piled in heaps where the cows languished in misery filled my nose even without the windows open. My life back in Inglewood with garbage bins piled high and the mess I was in could easily be compared and contrasted to these same conditions.

A few miles down the road was my new future, Fresno — the birthplace of the California Raisins, the 1980's dancing dolls who sang "I Heard It through the Grapevine."

Entering the city, I imagined the heat and dust settling inside my truck, taking up permanent residence. I could tell this was going to be a long August. I was miserable and had back sweat from my neck to the lower part of my butt. If this was to be an everyday occurrence during the summer months, I was in for a world of hurt.

I looked off the road toward the grapevines and envisioned a grape becoming a raisin and beginning to jig on the vine. Now I understood where the inspiration for the Dancing Raisins came from — heat exhaustion. Waking up from my reverie, I spotted a small white puppy on the side of the road. It must have gotten lost or been abandoned by someone. I made a U-turn and went back to find it. The poor pup didn't make things easy; it scurried under some brush. I coaxed her to come out with my half-eaten bologna sandwich, but she was still afraid.

I reached into the brambles, scratching my arms, and pulled the dog toward me. I sat with her in the dirt, whispering softly as cars whizzed by. She wore no dog tags and from the looks of her hadn't had a bath since birth. I named her Freeway since my creative juices were seeping out of me in this unbearable heat. I put her in the passenger seat of my truck, and we set off to start a new life together. It was late afternoon when I arrived, and the sun was high and hotter than it had been earlier.

Parking my truck on Baker Street next to the apartment complex that I rented unseen, I noticed a somewhat charming, cream stucco building that looked like an old Spanish mission. Made sense to me. This had once been a settled region of Spain. Most important to me, though, since this was where I would be spending the next four years of my life, was that the apartment was furnished and near the college.

I reluctantly opened the truck door, and Freeway and I raced inside to the air-conditioned rental office to pick up my keys. The office was clean looking but had a familiar smell of dust, the kind that smelled like it'd been caked on fan blades or on the back side of window blinds where people never took the time to clean.

The manager of the apartment complex handed me two keys. "You'll need to pay a pet fee for that dog," she said.

"No problem. How much for the deposit?"

"It's a hundred and fifty, and you'll get used to the heat," she said, eyeing the sweat running down my face.

I doubted I ever would. I handed her the cash, exited the office, and jumped back into my truck with Freeway in tow. After finding a better parking space, I walked up the sidewalk to our new apartment and opened the door. I peeked inside and saw it was furnished in shabby chic.

I dropped my purse on the kitchen counter and made a beeline for the bathroom, wiping sweaty hands on my jeans. I passed the air conditioner and saw the thermostat was set at ninety-seven degrees so I cranked it down as far as it could go to cool the place.

"There, Freeway; it's already getting better." After washing up a bit I wandered over to a cabinet, hoping there was some sort of container for my puppy to drink out of. No such luck, so I turned the water faucet on in the kitchen and held her over the sink. Poor thing. She swallowed as if she had never had water before.

After our water break, Freeway jumped into a chair, taking a seat next to the air conditioner, and held her face in the cooling air. I walked back into the heat and retrieved my belongings, unloaded my luggage onto the double bed, and put my clothes into the chest of drawers. I made a mental list of other things I would need — bedding for myself and a doggy bed for Freeway, food for us both, and other necessities.

Turning towards the kitchen, I checked to see if Freeway would brave the weather with me, but I soon learned that my puppy found the coolness of the apartment preferable to a foray into the heat. Smart girl! I begrudgingly left the cool apartment in search of a cheap box store to buy not so much what I wanted but what I needed.

The heat once again hit me hard, like opening an oven door only to find no cake on the other side. My hair was plastered to my face from the humidity. I couldn't even escape it in my truck.

Two types of people described to me what it was like to live in Fresno. The "glass half full" people spoke of how Fresno was the breadbasket of the world, and the "glass half empty" people described Fresno as the armpit of California where the crime was way above the national average. I think both groups were right, but I was going to be on the half full side and make the most of it.

I wanted to grow things; I wanted to bring something to life. I was tired of remembering death. So if Fresno was a bountiful breadbasket, that's where I wanted to be.

{ 7 }

"Wine makes daily living easier, less hurried with fewer tensions and more tolerance."
BENJAMIN FRANKLIN

I settled into my apartment, and the next day enrolled at California State University-Fresno.

Cal State Fresno was a pretty campus. It had a hundred species of trees and six other plants commonly used in the making of Native American baskets. It rested on one hundred and fifty acres, comprised of raisin and wine-grape vineyards. It also had a commercial fifty-thousand-gallon winery and a state-of-the-art processing facility.

There was a girl sitting under a maple tree in the Peace Garden eating her lunch. She was surrounded by flowers and a sparkling brook. She looked about my age with brilliant dark eyes. I sat near her and opened the lunch bag I packed with cheese sticks, peanut butter crackers, and water.

"Where are you from?" she asked.

She didn't start with How are you? That was unsettling.

The woman wore a bun at the back of her neck, and when she moved, little bits of hair loosened, forming wisps around her face. Her complexion was dark so I thought she was probably the outdoorsy type. I wondered if she hiked, owned a backpack, or something. Her clothes were casual, befitting a college student, but they weren't cheap. She wore jeans, a designer silk shirt, and expensive boots. She wore rings that didn't look like knock-offs, but then again, how would I know?

"Los Angeles." Nobody cared where I was from, but I hoped no one would find out about my past.

"Mmm, it's a busy city from what I hear," she said. There was no judgment; she had likely only heard about Los Angeles from the local news, which showed congested freeways, gangs, and murder.

"Where do you live?"

"I live and work at Waterford Horse Ranch up in Oakhurst for board and a few dollars to help me with food and gas," she answered.

"A horse ranch? That sounds exciting! I've never seen a horse or a cow for that matter. At least not in person. I'm sure there were farms in LA; I just never saw any of them."

"They don't have cows at the ranch. Just horses, a pig, peacocks, and an assortment of dogs, cats, and chickens."

"What high school did you graduate from?" I asked.

"Exeter High. From there I went into the military for a couple of years."

"Wow!"

She looked down at her smartphone and jumped up, still talking as she walked away. "Hey, I've got to go, but how about if I meet you here tomorrow, and we can talk more? What's your name?"

"Daisy Murphy," I shouted after her. "What's yours?"

"Katie Rodriguez."

After lunch, I finished registering for school and walked around to get a feel for what was to be my home for the next four years. I felt relaxed, and people smiled at me, unusual where I came from, particularly after the "incident."

I walked back to my apartment and picked up a pamphlet describing the courses I needed to take next semester to start my path towards becoming a winemaker. It was a hands-on learning program, and since I was a hands-on learner, that clicked.

Later that afternoon, Freeway and I strolled around the campus and found the grape vines students worked on all laid out in beautiful, well-tended rows. Further on, I happened upon a country store where students sold what they grew, from vegetables to freshly-butchered meat. They also had award-winning wine, ice cream, corn, and many other items that made my stomach growl. Maybe I could get a job there and be right on campus. I knew I had to find a job somewhere close to the apartment and Freeway.

All I wanted to do since being dragged off to Southern California was to run home to my dad and never look back. But now that I had this opportunity, I didn't want to find my dad. I didn't even remember what he looked like. My main worry was that I couldn't make it on my own and would end up back in my own personal hell.

So much of my youth had been sucked out of my life over the last several years, culminating in that final tragic moment ten years before. I lost so much of myself — that I would never be able to erase from my mind.

On the rare occasion when my mother and I spoke during my school years, she often said how like my father I was, how he'd never understood her either, and he was a scumbag bottom feeder like me. Or my favorite — that he and I were to blame for her horrible life. It was unfortunate that the only way I knew my dad was through her colorful terms of endearment.

Otherwise, I had scant memories of my father. He was out of the picture after I was about six years old and Mom got "sick." Every year he sent a card for my birthday with silver dollars in it — one for each year of my life. Of course, Mike took them away from me under the pretense that I was a "bad" girl who didn't deserve a gift. That's all I knew of my father, a few coins. Now I just wanted to live on my own, cutting off those familial ties. In order to do that, I needed to make it as a student … with a job.

Long before I became an official viticulturist I needed to know more about wine. I needed to buy books other than what was required for my classes, and I wanted to start my own experimental garden. I figured the more I knew, the better off I would be.

I read everything I found about grapes on the Internet and wrote everything down in the notebook I kept on viticulture. I even went to Vino's, a tasting room where I could buy a flight of wine for five dollars. The owner told me about a book everyone should own, *The Wine Bible*. I learned wine was more popular now than ever, and premium wines were produced and consumed all over the world. The opportunities for me were endless.

I decided to use the little backyard of my ground floor apartment to grow Pinot Noir. It would let me get some practice in before I bought my own winery someday in the future. I could study the growth, the texture, and trellis system. Who knows? Maybe I would create my own blend and call it The Grey Stallion.

Yes, still dreaming but I had hope.

{ 8 }

{at his first sip of champagne}
"come quickly! I am tasting stars!"
DOM PRIGNON

Every afternoon after my last class in microbiology, I went to Vino's to study. All the locals seemed to hang out there. Chuck, the owner, made a special corner for me, and it had a great atmosphere. The food was good, particularly the hamburgers, and everything was served with freshly-harvested apples, plums, and pears. It got pretty quiet in the afternoon, and that gave me a chance to observe many of the locals, including a lady who worked across the street at a hair salon and a doctor who just lost his wife of several years to cancer. There was a golf pro who was rather shy and never spoke a word to me, but I noticed that he did "down" several glasses of wine before going back to work.

It wasn't long before Chuck invited me to attend a wine tasting event. I met two guys, David Brinker and Hans Weizner, both on the high end of the wine business. I ended up making Vino's my second home with all of the interesting, down-to-earth people I met there.

I learned through Chuck that wine was defined many different ways, depending upon how it's used. People used wine all over the world to celebrate, as well as to add to the enjoyment of food and foster conversation. There were collectors who waited for the very moment that the wine hit its peak flavor, showing patience and restraint. Some bought wine merely to enjoy and experience the moment they were living in, others for its medicinal benefits. I wondered how these good people of Fresno would describe my mother's husband since his breakfast, lunch, and dinner were the malted wine "Ripple." Mike was definitely not a connoisseur of good taste.

Wine was written about by some of the world's best-known poets, authors, and playwrights. It was mentioned more than any other food or beverage in the Bible. I wanted to count how many times wine was listed there, but with all the work I was doing at school, there wasn't enough time. Whatever people's reasons for drinking, a better understanding of wine was going to give me something to talk about to the most discerning customer. That was a real plus for me if I got that job at the college's agricultural store.

I looked forward to visiting the local wineries. The last time I saw him at Vino's, Hans Weizner invited me to his place for a tour. I planned on visiting him on the weekend. The more the owners of the wineries got to know me, the better my odds were in landing an internship.

{ 9 }

*"Men are like wine — some turn to vinegar,
but the best improve with age."*
POPE JOHN XXIII

I closed the student Ag store for the evening and drove home for a bite to eat with Freeway and to prepare for my visit to Weingart Winery. The Internet was a great resource for information on Mr. Weizner, his family, his farm, and the wine he produced.

Weingart Winery was unique because of the natural spring water which provided the property with ten rain-fed ponds. Combined with the fertile soil and the vineyards growing in the foothills of the Sierra Nevada, it was easy to see why the wines of the vineyard fared so well in and around the county.

Saturday arrived, and Freeway and I were up early. After breakfast, we jumped into my truck and drove to Oakhurst where Weingart was located. I kept an eye on my phone so I could see the turn-off of Highway 41. I knew I had been here when I was young. On the left, something I remembered vividly was a beautiful old white church surrounded by carved headstones that settled comfortably buried in the earth where many of the original settlers were buried. It brought some sense of belonging to a place that I thought was perhaps taken away from me.

Forty-five minutes later we arrived at our destination. I jumped out and hit a button for entry through a magnificent wrought iron fence.

"You're early," Hans said, walking out of his villa to greet me.

"I hope I'm not too early," I said in earnest.

Waylaying my fears, Mr. Weizner took me and Freeway out to his fields of vines and showed us what he was growing.

"Why does Weingart grow only Bordeaux?" I asked out of curiosity. There were so many different types of grapes to choose from that I didn't understand why he limited himself.

"Nowadays, more attention is being paid to the individual vineyards, clonal selection, and the trellis system. We've become more careful in matching the grape variety with my specific site. The grape has done better in this soil, and with our natural water we never have to worry about the drought."

That information was useful to know for my future endeavor. I had worked on my patio on the trellis system. "How much pesticide is used on the grapes?" I knew I was asking too many questions. I saw it in his face; he was growing impatient.

"Sustainability has become the international buzz word in viticulture. Grape growers everywhere are using fewer herbicides and pesticides, and many are going organic. We are organic. We have far less filtering of wine, leading to a more complex and natural taste."

We meandered around his acreage where I saw many different buildings. I didn't want to ask him what each one was for. Finally we came to his tasting room where he sold many products to passing tourists who ventured out on the trails.

"Would you like lunch, Daisy?" I did, but I had imposed long enough.

"Thank you, Mr. Weizner, but we've taken up too much of your time already. I'll head back to Fresno and start studying for my next test."

"You are welcome, Daisy. I'll look forward to our next meeting."

I hoped that meant he would hire me for an internship. "Me, too. Bye, Mr. Weizner."

"Goodbye, Daisy."

{ 10 }

"I cook with wine;
sometimes I even add it to the food."
W.C. FIELDS

The next four years weren't as lonely in college as I thought they would be because Katie took me through some very difficult patches of loneliness, anxiety, test taking, and, yes, a few parties.

After four years of school, my hard work was finally paying off. The professor instructed us to find a placement at a winery, and he provided a list where, if chosen, I would spend a year's internship. I couldn't wait to call Katie and tell her.

Katie decided to celebrate by taking Freeway and me to the ranch where she worked; it was close to Weingart Winery, Mr. Weizner's place. The farm was on twenty acres and had been in the owner's family for generations. It was a show stable where they kept expensive horses, Saddlebreds, Hackney ponies, Quarter horses, and thoroughbreds. At least that's what Katie told me. Katie was the stable hand so she was gone most weekends, feeding and taking care of the horses and polishing the bridles and saddles. By night time she was exhausted.

We walked around the ranch, looking at the horses, feeding carrots and peppermints to them. When she saw someone she knew, she introduced me to them.

"Hi, Jack, this is Daisy. We attend Fresno State together. I'm showing her around because she knows zilch about horses. Daisy, this is my boss, Jack." Katie glanced at me and smiled.

That was an interesting smile, I thought. I'd have to ask her about it later. "Hi. Nice to meet you, Jack, and yes, I know zilch about horses. Do they have four or five hooves?" I smiled back at Katie.

As the day wore on, I felt comfortable there, and Jack seemed familiar to me. The wrap-around porch and the daisy bushes also seemed familiar. This place was like a memory in the back of my mind that I could not quite get a handle on. Maybe if I relaxed, it would come to me. Jack was very kind and even invited us to have lunch with him.

We sat down, looking out into the pastures where the horses were grazing. An old dog meandered up the stairs and laid beside my foot. I reached down and petted him. Freeway nuzzled closer under my arm, making sure I didn't forget her.

"Seems like you got yourself a friend," Jack said.

I nodded. "Yours, too. He's a nice dog." His tail began to wag back and forth. Dogs were trustworthy. Always there, waiting for you. All you needed to do was love them, feed them, and walk them. If you did, you had a friend for life. This dog seemed familiar as well. "What's his name?"

"My daughter named him Prince." Jack was smiling across the table at me. "What are you studying, Daisy?"

"I'm studying to be a viticulturist at Fresno State."

"There's a farm across the street that's been abandoned for years. The owner wanted to grow grapes and have a winery there."

Interested, I leaned forward and asked, "What happened?"

"Things changed, that's all," he said.

After lunch, Katie and I headed back to town.

"So what do you think of Jack, Daisy?"

"He seems like he's a good boss to work for."

"Yeah, I know that, but what do you think of him?"

Confused by the question, I cocked my head, thinking. "He seems cool…" I shrugged. I wasn't sure what she wanted for an answer, but I think I gave her one that she liked because she smiled and became quiet. Driving past the rolling pastures was mesmerizing, and I found myself daydreaming of what my future would bring. Wouldn't it be awesome to own that farm across from Jack's? I could only hope!

{ 11 }

"Wine is life."
PETRONIUS

At about two a.m. I was still studying for a test I had to take the next day. My phone rang, which was a crazy time for someone to call.

"Hello?"

"Daisy, are you awake?" Katie asked.

"Yep. I've been studying the biosynthesis of grape-based compounds through fundamental chemical concepts of wine production and aging." I swiped the hair off my head. "In other words, you're a welcome distraction."

"I was visiting my boyfriend at a winery. While I was walking back to Jack's, I noticed some men unloading a whole bunch of barrels and bottles out of a storage unit. When they saw me, they began to run toward me. I took off toward Jack's. I'm hiding behind some bushes. I'm afraid to go to my room; I have a bad feeling about this."

"Do you know who they were?"

"I've seen them do this before, and I think I recognize some of them. If anything happens to me, Daisy, I have some letters and a diary in my trunk at the ranch. Please get them to the police."

"What's going on, Katie? I'm worried about you. Look, we can talk as long as you want or for the rest of the night. I'll stay right here with you."

"No, I'm all right now. It looks like they're gone but thanks. I think I'll talk to Jack about what I saw. He's a good guy, treats me like I'm his daughter. Bye."

Later that morning a policewoman knocked on my door. I rolled out of bed, still groggy from studying all night and clueless about what was going on. "Hello?"

"Daisy Murphy?"

"Yes," I said opening the front door.

"I'd like to ask you a few questions."

"Umm, okay. What's this about?"

"Do you know a Katie Rodriguez?"

"Yes."

"When was the last time you heard from or saw her?"

I gasped. "Is Katie okay?"

"Please answer the question, miss."

"I talked to her very early this morning. What's going on?"

"Do you know where Katie was when you spoke with her?"

"She said she was walking back to Jack Mendez's ranch and noticed something suspicious, barrels being unloaded by a nearby neighbor, so she called me because she was afraid. I said I'd stay on the phone all night, but she said she wanted to get back home and talk to Jack this morning."

"Your friend is missing, and a ranch hand was found dead. Katie dropped her phone so we learned you were the last person she spoke to. Any information you can share will be appreciated."

I shook my head. "Katie would never do anything wrong. Remember, she called me to report something going on."

I didn't know what Katie had seen, and I was glad she didn't drag me into the mess. Being questioned by police was closer than I wanted to be to another murder.

The routine of my life, my classes, work, studying and walks with Freeway seemed to slow down after Katie's disappearance. I wished I knew what happened to her that night. I didn't know what kind of trouble she was in, but it was obviously serious.

Thinking about Katie, Freeway and I walked to the row of mailboxes at the apartment complex to see what bills or ads came. Neither. Instead, someone sent an anonymous letter.

> Don't think you can get away from me by moving, Daisy.
> We're tied together for as long as you live.

Oh, God. Who could this be? No matter what I did to better myself or my life, I would always have Mike's murder hanging over my head. I should go to the police and report this. Who could know about this? Was it my mom? Would she really do this to me?

I headed to the bank with Freeway in tow. After standing in line for what seemed like hours, I finally got to the teller. I picked up a slip to deposit my paycheck from the college grocery store but then dropped it. The teller picked it up, and after depositing the money and giving me back a receipt, she looked at me funny. Before I slipped the receipt into my purse I looked to see if the amount was correct.

Holy shit! There was over one million dollars in my bank account. I glanced back at the teller. "Are you sure this is correct? I'm a student. I don't have this kind of money."

"Yes, ma'am; the amount is correct." The teller checked the computer screen. "The deposit was made in our Oakhurst branch."

"I'd like to withdraw all of the money." The teller gave me a quizzical look.

"I will need to make arrangements with the bank president for that large an amount. Come back tomorrow after twelve so he can discuss it with you."

I walked away with mixed feelings. I had money for the first time in my life but was terrified because I had no idea where it came from or who was connected. Once I got my hands on it, I had to hide this money somewhere in case whoever put it in wanted it back.

{ 12 }

*"He who aspires to be a serious wine drinker
must drink claret."*
SAMUEL JOHNSON

I drove back to school and went to the enology and viticulture department to speak with the department chair. I had to talk to someone about the money in my account. It had to be a mistake but why me? I didn't know anyone with a million dollars to spare.

Walking into the professor's office, I forgot about the million for a moment. Dr. Bishop said, "Daisy, have you decided on an internship at one of the wineries?"

"The only winery that matters to me is Weingart Winery. Hans Weizner owns it. I know him from Vino's so hopefully I have an in with him." Maybe I shouldn't say anything about the money and wait for someone to claim it. But what if I get caught?

"Here's a list of other possible internship sites just in case Weingart doesn't pan out. You can begin calling people from the list for an interview."

"Okay, thanks!" But my heart was still on Weingart's as I headed out the door.

Mr. Weizner was rumored to be a former music publisher and part of a very wealthy family in Munich. At Vino's, one afternoon, he told me that his family manufactured high-end eyeglasses.

"Can you really become a millionaire from selling eye wear?" I asked him the next time I saw him.

He told me he was once a professor and intimated that he made a fortune on the stock market. He then asked me about my life growing up. I quickly changed the subject.

I sat quietly in his office waiting for him to return to interview me. His assistant Charlotte told me he was out looking over his vines. If I got the internship, I would be learning from one of the best vintners in the area.

I gazed out at the vineyards, picking my cuticles, a nervous habit I acquired and needed to stop. I wanted this job, and his fields were impressive. I was so intent that I jumped out of my seat when he walked through the door.

"I hope I'm not too late for our interview, Daisy."

"Not at all, Mr. Weizner. I enjoyed looking out at the fields."

"I enjoy this view myself and please call me Hans," he said, glancing out the window. "I remember from our conversations at Vino's that you have a good knowledge base about grapes. I also know a friend of yours, Katie Rodriguez. She worked at a ranch about two miles away."

"Katie? You know Katie?"

"I haven't seen her in a while," he said, shaking his head. "It's sad; she was a good kid. I attended a candlelight vigil in town for her. I haven't heard anything lately about her disappearance. Do you know if the police ever found out what happened to her?"

"No, I was interviewed but haven't heard anything about her since," I responded.

"Daisy, I'd like to take a chance on you so your education as a viticulturist begins at Weingart today."

"You mean I got the internship?" When he nodded, I pulled out my recorder pen and jotted down a few notes while he talked. I had to make sure I didn't forget anything, and I had a thousand more questions that he patiently answered.

"Daisy, something the school doesn't teach is that wine quality has improved substantially, and in Madera County where Oakhurst is located they have been making wine for over two hundred years.

"I learned everything I could about the science and technology of winemaking, both through school and visiting the wineries. Growers now have readapted back-to-the-earth farming techniques like they once used, organic farming."

"I'm sure it has, Mr. Weizner, sorry Hans. That's exactly why I'm here." Never hurts to butter up the boss.

"I'd like you to work with Charlotte in my wine tasting room. You'll get an excellent beginning to your education from her at our winery."

"Thanks, Hans. Can I start now? I'll go help your clients." I studied every day at Vino's and watched the owners help consumers with wine so I knew what he wanted me to do. I thought that I was more educated than a regular college student, and previously I worked at a winery in Inglewood.

In the Weingart's tasting room I was in my element. My old cheer leading days made me a natural in people skills.

I wanted to impress Charlotte, but as I turned to greet a client and offer her a taste of wine, I tripped and fell into Mrs. Wright. "I'm so sorry," I said. Charlotte gave me a if looks could kill stare of disapproval. I began again, "Excuse me, Mayor." I met Mrs. Wright at Vino's not long ago.

"The Bordeaux is exceptional here at Weingart's, Daisy. But I'm having guests over tonight, and I'm looking for a white wine."

"Have you tried the new wines we just got in — Butter or Epiphany?"

"Thank you, Daisy. I heard of a couple of new ones." She straightened her dress that I'd twisted in the fall.

"We also have a wonderful Chenin Blanc that we just uncorked. Try this and then I have a special treat — a Viognier."

As Mrs. Wright tasted the Butter wine, I wandered over to help Mr. Billingsly. I introduced myself, luckily without tripping this time.

"Hello. My name is Daisy, and if I can be of any help selecting a wine, please let me know."

"Why do you have screw caps on your wine instead of corks?"

"They seal the wine much better than corks," I answered. I had taken the corks versus screws class and was glad I could use my knowledge.

He was a heavy-set man, already sweating inside the wine tasting room.

"How much chaptalization is done here"?

"Ahh, you're very knowledgeable." I grimaced, hoping I was going to get it right. "Vintners rarely add sugar anymore."

I hoped he wouldn't ask any more questions. There was only so much I could remember while being observed by Charlotte.

"Can I offer you a Gamay Pinot Noir? It's low in tannin and lighter in color. We received a new bottle. I think you'll enjoy it."

"Yes, thank you. That's exactly what I came to buy."

Smiling, I handed over the sale to Charlotte, who continued to glare at me but rang the wine up at a hefty price.

Hans smiled and approached me. "Your first day is quite a success. If every day is like this, you'll have a permanent job when you graduate."

"Thank you, Mr. Weizner," I gushed. "Thank you for giving me this opportunity."

"You're welcome. See that you make good use of what you're about to learn here." He winked.

"Oh, I will. I promise." I hoped he meant in regard to wine.

A woman walked in. Charlotte called out to her. "Hi, Marcie; the new girl will help you." That was me. Cool.

After one year of interning at Weingart, I was ready to graduate from the university. I was so excited. But there was that note that kept seeping back into my mind. And the million dollars. Could everything I worked so hard for disappear? I didn't kill Mike. I helped my mom and then called the police.

First, I needed to impress Hans without tripping or falling and help him make his new wine a success at the grand gala that he had prepared us all for. Then I might someday be recognized as a true vintner.

{ 13 }

"Nothing makes the future look so rosy as to contemplate it through a glass of Chambertin."
NAPOLEON

Madera Sheriff's Office

A little before eight-thirty on a sunny Monday morning in May, Detective Jake Frisco walked through the front door, passing the sergeant at the duty desk.

"Hey, Frisco! Want a donut?" He held one up.

"Tempting, Sergeant, especially with crumbs falling all over me." Frisco shook his head. "Any chance Marcie is brewing a new pot of coffee?"

"I am, Frisco," Marcie piped in.

Frisco headed into the central office in the back. Detective Sanchez was already grabbing the second donut before he finished his first. "No donut?" he asked.

"Nah, you can have mine."

"Why thank you, Frisco. How's your daughter?"

"She's good." Coffee in hand, Frisco left the break room and headed into his office. He had a busy day ahead, looking into the two-year-old unsolved disappearance of a young woman from Fresno State. He kept a picture of her on his desk to remind him that everyone mattered. He also had a deposition to deliver to the court and endless paperwork.

Just as he was about to head to the courthouse, Marcie came through his office door.

"What can I do for you, Marcie?" Frisco asked.

"For starters, you can relax a little." She smiled.

"I'll give that a try. Maybe tomorrow."

"I just met a young woman at Hans Weizner Estate in his wine tasting room. She helped me choose a bottle of wine and gave me a ticket to attend one of Hans Weizner's extravaganzas. I can't go, and since you like wines I figured you'd like to go."

He waited for her to tell him that she was joking; it didn't come. His wife left him last year, and ever since that day Marcie and his daughter Savannah tried to set him up on dates. So far he declined each and every one, but this time he was interested. Not for a date but he'd always wanted to see what Hans's estate looked like and certainly wanted to try some of his more exclusive wines that he couldn't afford on a detective's salary.

"Sure, I'll go."

"It's not a date, Frisco; she was just nice. I'm sure she could help you choose a wine."

"Great." The woman had interesting insights into the world of wine. Maybe Savannah and Marcie were right. He needed to get out more.

"I can't believe it's been a year since I really had a conversation with a woman unless you count the drug addicts and prostitutes, but I'm going for the wine."

"Um, hello? I'm sitting right in front of you. We're talking, and I'm a woman, remember? You're such a charmer."

"You know what I mean. I don't know if I'm ready to date, but I've always wanted to go to one of Hans's tastings and see his wine collection so this is the perfect opportunity."

"The young lady's name is Daisy. She'll be working and already at the party, helping Hans show guests around, etc."

"Great, what does she look like?"

"She'll find you. I showed her a picture of all of us at the staff picnic last year and told her you have an interest in wine."

"Thanks, Marcie," he said, taking hold of the ticket. "I'll see you tomorrow. I'm on my way to the courthouse."

{ 14 }

"No nation is drunken where wine is cheap, and none sober where the dearness of wine substitutes ardent spirits as the common beverage."
THOMAS JEFFERSON

Oakhurst, California is a pleasant community, and the soil is incredible for growing wine. I could see myself settling down and building my own winery one day and spending the rest of my life growing grapes and basking in the warmth of this beautiful, small town.

Hans arrived early to work Friday morning. He asked me to observe his sommelier, Andrew Speck, at the wine tasting party that night. It was to be a weekend-long affair attended by wine critics, retailers, various local celebrities, city council members, and the mayor.

A sommelier was a job I was interested in knowing more about, but the only thing that made learning the job rough was the sommelier was never around. His unreliability put Hans on edge, but then again a Master Sommelier was hard to come by in a small town like Oakhurst.

After setting up the tables and wine glasses for the party, I stepped into the front gardens of Hans's home for the first time, and it was overwhelming in a very good way. Hans spared no expense to show his clientele who owned the top local winery. Tonight he would open scores of old and rare wines, all provided at his own expense, and serve everyone in custom-made "Weizner" glasses supplied by his friend and famous glass maker Georg Ritz. I was looking for Hans when Charlotte saw my confusion and came over to ask if I needed help.

"Yes, I was wondering if you have seen Hans?"

"Sorry I haven't." Just as she finished her sentence, Mr. Weizner came up through the cellar door.

He was impeccably dressed and expected all of his employees to be dressed well. He even gave us the name of some boutiques in Fresno where we could buy our clothes and what he expected us to wear for the weekend. I had money, that was for sure, but I kept it safely squirreled away until the time I really needed it. I had money from my job at the school agricultural store set aside for emergencies but not for clothes so I had to find a local Second Chance clothing store to purchase a dress. I found a beautiful one in black with white lace peonies covering the top half, flowing down into a black gown with an open back.

As I entered the mezzanine, Hans walked over and glanced appreciatively at me.

"Are you ready for this evening, Daisy?"

"Yes, sir."

"Good because I have yet to see Andrew."

"What do you mean?"

Snapping back at me, he said, "Andrew is nowhere to be found."

"Oh, okay." I wondered where Andrew was. He knew how important this event was to Hans.

{ 15 }

"Gentlemen, in the little moment that remains to us between the crisis and the catastrophe, we may as well drink a glass of champagne."
PAUL CLAUDEL

Guests began arriving promptly at 6:30 that night. As they walked in through the front door, two staff members greeted them and took their coats.

Another staff member ushered them in to keep the line moving toward Mr. Weizner. He greeted each person by name and lavished them with praise.

While speaking with his guests, Hans made no secret of having produced an incredible wine. Not that it would have been easy to do so. *Wine Magazine* had made him a celebrity in the wine world since the record sale to Corbe's. He greeted each guest and spoke in earnest about his fine bottles of wine. It was a 2000 Mission de Madonna Noire and sold for twelve thousand dollars a bottle.

"Someday you'll have to tell me about the process that was used to make 2000 so much better than 1999. How many barrels did you make?" I asked Hans.

"Enough talk. You have work to do, right?"

"Yes, sir."

"Good." That was a cold brush off, and it confused me.

Shaking off the memory of that interaction and the many others I had with Mr. Weizner lately, I decided to take a walk around the premises to see to the final touches. Taking a stroll toward the kitchen, I was serenaded by two lovely bands and couldn't help but smell the finely-prepared food by Oakhurst's own Crown Paella. Opening the door, I saw Andrew running toward the main house with Charlotte not far behind. I wondered what was going on between the two.

Romance? I doubted it.

{ 16 }

"Life is too short to drink cheap wine."
ANONYMOUS

Entering the gates to Weingart, Frisco saw it was a fancy party and was grateful to Savannah for insisting he not wear jeans and a tee shirt.

As he followed the long driveway to the estate, a kid approached his truck door and knocked on his window. Rolling it down, he looked at the kid who appeared to be eager to please.

"Can I park your truck for you, sir? Hey, this is a real classic! It's an open cab Model A. Wow, this is really upscale."

"Thanks, kid," he said, getting out of his one luxury purchase. He handed over the keys and walked up the stairs. He had never been to Mr. Weizner's home and winery. He admired its Mediterranean style. The gardens were full of water fountains painted in gold paint. There was a gazebo and a koi fishpond. No expense seemed to be spared, and he was impressed. He was wandering around the gardens when he saw a tall blonde cleaning some wine glasses. She wasn't exactly beautiful, but there was something about her, a mystery within a mystery. Boy, he was glad he wore a nice suit.

"Hello?" Frisco said.

"Hello," the woman said with a smile.

"My name is Frisco."

Grinning, she said, "Hello, Frisco. My name is Daisy. I thought I recognized you from the picture Marcie showed me."

"You have a good memory. This place looks incredible."

"It does. I'm heading into the party and would love to talk with you about your interest in wine. Follow me and I'll get you a monogrammed glass. Ready to go?" She was distracting with those light blue eyes. He frowned and wondered how this night was going to go.

"Sure, I can't wait."

Upon entering the front door, they were greeted by a waiter offering Sauvignon Blanc, a versatile white wine, to start the evening. After Frisco received a glass, Daisy ushered him into the banquet room with all the other guests.

"So what do you do here?" he asked, trying to start up a conversation.

"I'm a viticulturist. I just finished my internship here at the winery. Mr. Weizner invited me to observe his wine tasting party and help out if I'm needed. Tomorrow I start my first day as a viticulturist," Daisy proudly said. "What do you do, Frisco?"

"I'm a detective for Madera County."

"Oh, that's right. Marcie told me you're also interested in the wine business."

"I decided to try this out. Who knows if I'd ever get to come to an event like this again. What brings you here to Oakhurst?"

"Good question." Daisy headed to the hors d'oeurve table without answering. Definitely a riddle within a puzzle. Just my kind. Frisco smiled.

A soft clanking sound emanated from the front of the room. "Who likes wine?" Hans asked.

Everyone raised their glass. "If you are alert to the wine you drink, what it embodies, then you are alert to life," Hans said.

Greeting Dave Brinker, a competitor of his who owned the Montclaire winery just up the road, Hans said, "Let's play a game." Everyone began clinking their glasses. "You're up first, Dave. Tell us about the wine you are drinking."

"A game? Sounds interesting," Daisy said.

"If you're into that kind of thing." Frisco shrugged, worried that he'd be called upon, and he didn't know that much about wine.

"Since we're here at a wine tasting party, shouldn't we be?"

"Not necessarily, but then again …."

"You don't know what your kind of thing is," I said, finishing his sentence with a smirk on my face. "Dave is a local vintner."

"He used to be a sheriff," Frisco said.

This surprised me. I was surrounded by cops, and it wasn't good. What if I slipped up? What if they had a wanted poster of my mom on a wall somewhere in the sheriff's office and recognized our shared last names? However, maybe I would be safer knowing these guys if the person who wrote the note came for me.

Hans wet his finger and rubbed it around the ring of his class, which made a screeching sound to get the guests' attention.

"Let me see," Dave said. "It's a Chardonnay; it has a chalky taste to it, probably from the soil it's grown in. It is a noble grape because of its ability in growing the greatest dry wines in the world. Last, but far from least, it's an oak wine."

"Very good," our host smiled through clenched teeth. "Who's up for our next challenge?"

No one raised their hand. Probably because no one wanted to look like an idiot. I certainly didn't.

Frisco raised his hand. I couldn't believe it; I had no idea he was a connoisseur of wine.

"Hello. And you are?" Hans asked.

"Name's Frisco."

Hans walked over to Andrew who had just walked into the mezzanine, ignoring Frisco. I edged closer to Hans and could hear him whisper to Charlotte that bottles were missing and something about wine labels. Hans cleared his throat and asked, "Are you up for the next challenge?"

"Sure, but I was volunteering my new acquaintance." Frisco looked at me and grinned.

I was fuming, and I'm sure Frisco could feel it. What if I messed up in front of Mr. Weizner?

"Andrew," a voice said as he walked down the cellar stairs.

Startled by the voice coming from behind a wine barrel, Andrew gulped, "Hello."

"I hear congratulations are in order."

"What do you mean?"

"I think you know."

"Who's there? What do you want?"

"You've been stealing wine, Andrew. First, you date that bitch, Katie. And now you're trying to leave me."

Afraid that he was found out, Andrew began to shake. "No, that's not true. I was just waiting for the right time to pay you."

"Who else is a part of this little scheme of yours?"

"What are you talking about?"

The figure stepped forward and plunged a knife into Andrew's chest between the third and fourth ribs, the closest route to the heart. He stiffened in a spasm of shock and pain, choking sounds emanating from between his lips.

The murderer walked away smiling as a rag was used to wipe bloody hands. Andrew's crumpled body was left at the foot of the stairs.

{ 17 }

"Clearly, the pleasures of wine afforded are transitory but so are the ballet, or a musical performance. Wine is inspiring and adds greatly to the joy of living."

NAPOLEON

Ladies and gentlemen, this is my ex-intern and newest employee, Daisy Murphy, a graduate from the Fresno State Enology & Viticulturist program. Let's all welcome her with a round of applause."

I looked at the sea of people, all eyes on me as I stepped up to where our host stood. "Thank you, Mr. Weizner." As Hans handed me the mystery glass, I glanced sideways at Frisco and not in a friendly way.

"Okay, Daisy, let's play. What's in the wine glass?"

I swirled the liquid, mesmerized by the color and the smell. "It is a Sauvignon Blanc. It's a white variety with a very distinctive character. It's high in acidity and has a pronounced aroma and flavor. Besides herbaceous notes, Sauvignon Blanc wines display mineral aromas and flavor, vegetal character, or in certain climates fruity character, such as ripe melon, figs, or passion fruit. The wines are light to medium bodied and dry or dryish. Most of them are unoaked. In my particular case this Sauvignon is from California, unoaked, and has a fruity characteristic." I looked at Frisco's face. I guess he thought he was going to be the bell of the ball, but nope, it was me.

"Daisy, you really know your wine." There was a hint of surprise in Hans's voice.

"Thank you, sir," I said, blushing.

Turning away from me he said to the elite, "And now we're heading to the wine tasting room down in the cellar where I have a special treat, Russian Caviar. Ladies and gentlemen, games are over, and a new game is about to begin. Bring your wine glasses as I will be sharing my exceptional wine from the Weingart Winery. I hope you liked the game, Daisy," Hans said.

"Yes, sir."

"You are quite a surprise, young lady. And I finally found Andrew. I sent him downstairs to set up the wine station. Get down to the cellar before the guests and see if you can be of assistance to him. I want everything to turn out well."

Rounding the corner, I stepped down the cellar stairs toward the wine barrels and tripped over what looked like a bag of clothes and landed next to an oak barrel. Getting back up, I reached over for the lights, and oh, my God, it was Andrew. He looked dead. I shoved him with my foot and saw the large pool of blood underneath him and his eyes open and vacant. He was definitely dead.

Shit, shit, shit! What was I going to do? Sweat poured down my face. This would be a disaster for Hans. I raced back up the stairs to stop the guests from coming down. I grabbed Hans by his arm.

"He's dead," I whispered as discreetly as I could.

"Who's dead?"

"Andrew, sir."

"Nonsense. He probably got drunk and collapsed. I'll call an ambulance."

This was an important evening for Hans. He stopped everyone from proceeding down to the cellar. "Attention, everyone. There will be a slight delay. Charlotte, bring some caviar and toast for our guests."

I looked at my shoes that had blood on the sides, at the ceiling, at the people, anywhere except at Hans.

As soon as I spotted Frisco on the stairs, I walked over and told him what I found. He handed me his wine glass, then ran down and found Andrew's body next to the wine barrels.

Taking control of the scene, he pulled his cell phone out and made a call to the precinct, informing them of the situation.

Upstairs in the banquet room, a guest asked if there was a problem with the wine. There were rumors spreading, and a pervading tension came upon the group. I was already tense.

Frisco came through the cellar door and with a calmer and less commanding voice said, "Unfortunately, we will not be drinking any more wine this evening." The guests, as if they were all connected by the same neuron, gasped at the same time.

"There is a team of law enforcement on the way. Everyone, you need to get comfortable; it's going to be a long night."

A stout woman with a black bun and long, red lacquered nails said in a snooty voice, "I'm unable to stay, detective, as I have another function to attend."

"Wasn't this supposed to be a weekend event? Sorry, we need to account for everyone's whereabouts this evening. You all need to stay until we clear you."

She was not satisfied with Frisco's response.

"Clear us for what?"

"Just stay put," Frisco ordered, the palm of his hand in the air. He called for an ambulance. Everyone at the party wanted to leave. Rumors spread that someone was dead, and the group began to pepper Frisco with questions. No one wanted to get mixed up with a murder.

I wrung my hands and reached for something to hold myself upright. I couldn't believe this was happening when everything was going so right.

The paramedics and sheriff were at the scene in less than twenty minutes, but in that short amount of time, the impatience of the guests grew exponentially. Frisco kept his cool at all times. I watched him, trying to figure out what to do with my hands. A reminder of my past life that I wanted to erase from my mind came rushing in all at once.

"What do we have, Frisco?" Sanchez asked. I looked at the sergeant. He was fifty years old but looked more like seventy. He had been through the ringer.

"A murder — there's a knife wound," he said as a matter of fact.

Frisco introduced Sergeant Sanchez to me. "Have you always worked in Madera?" I asked nervously.

"I used to work in Los Angeles. I moved here to get away from crime in the big city," he answered. Little do you know that Madera has its own share of crime statistics, I thought.

Frisco turned to his partner and said, "Follow me." Both detectives headed back down to the cellar.

Frisco asked, "Sanchez, you got gloves on you?"

"Yeah but use them wisely. I don't have any more."

As the detectives descended, the forensics team followed. Frisco made it known that he was a guest at the event and therefore his latent prints would be all over the crime scene. He stopped in front of the wooden barrel where Andrew lay in a crumpled heap.

"Check the scene. See if there is anything suspicious or evidence we can collect."

"Are we assuming that one of the people or persons upstairs is the suspect?"

"Totally possible."

"What do we know so far?"

Frisco smiled and bluntly said, "Not much."

"You were here; do you have any idea who these people are?"

"We were all upstairs, at least all that I know of." He turned, giving me a suspicious look. "Sanchez, I've got to call home and let the neighbor know I'll be late and then talk to my daughter. Give me a minute."

Frisco walked back upstairs to make his phone call and noticed that the uniformed officers were getting the basic information from the guests and employees. He left to make that phone call.

{ 18 }

"Wine cheers the sad, revives the old, inspires the young, makes weariness forget his toll."
LORD BYRON

Captain Ochoa walked through the entry door and began inspecting the scene. From time to time he spoke to different members of the tight community.

Detective Frisco walked over to Sanchez and silently asked him to get a subpoena for bank accounts for Andrew and Hans Weizner.

"Frisco, I'd like to have a word with you in private," Ochoa said.

"Yes, sir."

"You need to handle this case delicately. We have a number of influential people here."

"As soon as we get finished with our inspection, the coroner leaves, and we've processed everyone here, we will let everyone go."

"See to it."

"Yes, sir."

{ 19 }

*"I love everything that's old: old friends, old times, old
manners, old books, old wine."*
OLIVER GOLDSMITH

Early the next morning Frisco arrived home after a long night spent at the
Weingart Winery. He entered the kitchen through the back door and saw his
daughter at the breakfast table with Sue Lynn, the neighborhood babysitter,
eating blueberry pancakes at the table. "Thanks for staying the night, Sue
Lynn. I owe you."

"Savannah and I had a great time. Would you like some pancakes?" She
pointed to the stove.

"Tempting but I need to shower and get back to the police station."

"Hey, Dad, tell us about the party."

"Let me get you a cup of coffee first," Sue Lynn offered.

"Come on, give me the juicy details," Savannah pleaded.

"Not so good. I'm never going out again."

"Why?"

"I volunteered a new female acquaintance named Daisy who works for the
winery for a quiz game of sorts. She had to name a wine from a myriad of
different wines that were in a paper bag."

"That wasn't the smartest thing to do, Dad. What if she messed up? That
would've been disastrous for her in front of his friends and guests."

"I hadn't thought of that," he said sheepishly. "I won't be seeing her again
anyway. We weren't a good fit."

"I've seen Daisy while I was walking to school by the old Tuscan Villa. We
talked about the horses next door. She seemed nice."

"I'll hand you that, Savannah. And I did embarrass her, but she came off
looking good in front of all the guests."

"Dad, you've got to get out there. Maybe Daisy wasn't comfortable. She is
new to this town. Plus, you're not the easiest person to get along with."

"Who says? Ya know you're a little too old for your ten years." He smiled.

"I hate to butt in, but here's the coffee." Sue Lynn handed him a cup. "I
gotta go."

"I thought you might. Let's go into my office. It's a little more private, and you can ask all the questions you like," Weizner said nervously.

"I'm really sorry about this, Mr. Weizner," Frisco said while gazing at all the paintings and sculptures on the walls as they walked to Hans's office.

"Please, call me Hans. Has anyone called his wife yet?"

"Yes, our office called after the coroner finished," Frisco said.

"I should call her as well," Hans said.

I was outside Hans's office, listening around the corner. I wanted to know more about my employer and the death of my predecessor. Okay, I was eavesdropping.

"Why did you hire Daisy? And how long has she been employed with you?" Frisco questioned.

"She has been studying the wine industry for the last few years, and she's good. And what, if anything, does the murder of Andrew have to do with me employing Daisy as my new viticulturist? Do you think she's a suspect?"

Wait, I was a suspect now? What if they dug into my past and found out about my mother and what she had done? Guilt by association? God, I hoped not. Things were just beginning to look up for me.

Frisco asked, "Anything else you think that might help with finding the murderer, give me a call."

"Honestly, I can't think of anyone who would kill Andrew. He was a little irresponsible but nothing to kill over."

"All right, thanks, Mr. Weizner."

I heard footsteps coming toward me. I quickly walked around the corner, bumping into Frisco and acted as if I was surprised. I didn't think he'd leave Hans's office so fast.

"I need you to come down to the station."

"Another date? Why? Our last one went so well."

"No, it wasn't a date. I got a ticket to an event; that's it," he said chagrined. "I need to ask you a few questions at the precinct."

"Why not here?"

"Why can't you do as I ask?"

"Why do you ask stupid questions?"

"I could cuff you."

"I don't do that until the third date." One look at Frisco's face changed my attitude. "Okay, I'm coming. I just need to tell Mr. Weizner that I'm going with you."

"Fine but make it fast."

"Why?" I questioned.

"Are we going to go through this dance again?"

"Depends." I really needed to learn how to stop talking.

"Knock it off and let's go. I have my orders so this wasn't my idea." He growled.

"Then whose was it?" Oh, my God, if looks could kill. "Okay, I'll shut up," I said, jumping into my truck. "I can drive, right? I'm not arrested or anything."

"That's fine, I'll meet you there."

{ 21 }

"(Making wine) is like having children;
you love them all, but boy, are they different."
BUNNY FINKLESTEIN

Frisco left Freeway and me in his office and walked into the captain's office. "Captain Ochoa, I don't think it's a good idea," I overheard Frisco say.

While seated at Frisco's desk I eavesdropped at Frisco and the captain's conversation and observed the precinct. It was old, probably built in the early 1900s. The flooring was Formica. It was puke green and curled up on the edges. It reminded me of the precinct in Inglewood ten years before. I began to get an ache in my stomach thinking about it. At this point I was hoping I wouldn't need a paper bag. I was feeling nauseous and didn't want to add any more color to the already grungy flooring.

I took notice of the lack of organization; a person suffering from obsessive-compulsive disorder would be on the floor in a fetal position as soon as that person walked in through the door. There was paper strewn about the place, not to mention the number of paper coffee cups stacked on all the desks. Do these people know that there is such a thing as a reusable cup?

The only thing that was remotely relaxing in the police station was a picture of an aerial view of Madera County. The amount of acreage dedicated to farming was crazy good. Slowly I breathed in and out, finally calming myself.

As the time ticked away, I surmised that most of the suspects probably confessed to a crime they didn't commit just so they didn't have to sit on these wooden chairs any longer. My butt was going numb. I wanted out of this wasteland they called an office. I stood up and walked from Frisco's desk into the captain's office.

They looked surprised at my interruption. "Hello. My name is Daisy Murphy. You must be Captain Ochoa. I've heard so many good things about you, and honestly, I've been listening to your conversation." I said that with a smile and turned my head slightly to smirk at Frisco.

"I don't think eavesdropping is usually a good idea, Daisy. May I call you that?"

"Of course," I said.

Frisco looked at me puzzled.

"I've checked your school records. You're knowledgeable about the wine industry, and now that Hans Weizner has hired you to work as the viticulturist, I think you would be a great consultant for our department in this case." He glanced over at Frisco.

"I really don't need her. I've worked cases without a consultant before," Frisco said.

"Duly noted but not in the food and wine industry. This is a big part of our tourism; we can't afford to screw this up. I think Daisy," he turned and smiled at me, "would be very helpful, and she already works at the winery. Maybe we can find out who was stealing the wine labels, and that could lead you to who murdered Andrew."

Scowling, Frisco turned to walk away.

"See you tomorrow, Frisco," I called after him. I turned and shook Captain Ochoa's hand, but before I could leave, he held me back. "I looked into all the allegations of abuse and possible molestation in Inglewood where you're originally from."

I looked at the captain, and my insides felt like they were going to fall out. I went stone cold but said through clenched teeth, "It's in the past."

A past that just won't stay dead, I thought.

"We are going to need to talk about your mother's husband and your mother's disappearance."

I was afraid it would come up, just not so soon. I began to shake, not from the cold but from complete fear. "I don't know where my mother is; she just left me and took off to God knows where."

"And your missing college friend, Katie? A friend of my wife teaches at the college and remembers the murder of a groom at a horse ranch."

"I reported that to the police. Katie did call me. She was frightened but said she would be fine. I wish I knew what happened to her. She was like a sister to me for the four years we were in school together." God, I was tired of the past haunting me in life and in my dreams. Make that nightmare.

The captain leaned forward as if to say something more but stopped. "You can go now."

I walked out of the station's front door. I needed a drink. I pushed the hair out of my face as I got into my truck and leaned over the steering wheel, my mind racing. Had my mother been found and said something to the police? I began wheezing.

{ 22 }

*"My only regret in life is that I
did not drink more champagne."*
JOHN MAYNARD KEYNES

The next morning, after a good night's rest, I brushed my hair out of my face and decided I wasn't going to let today end as yesterday had. The sun was filtering through the blinds of my bedroom window at the Chateau Inn in Oakhurst that I'd checked into the night before. It'd been too late to go home, and I had brought Freeway to work with me so it worked out perfectly. As I threw the bed covers off me, there was a knock on the door.

"Who's there?" I shouted.

"It's Frisco. Time to go."

So much for my vow about the day. Today was going to be no different than yesterday.

"I brought you some coffee from Café Java and a croissant."

I almost squealed with joy. The croissants were light and flaky, the coffee absolutely incredible. "You really shouldn't have. Did you bring some peach jam to go with it?" I opened the door.

"The girl at the bakery said you would ask for that, and yes, I did." He handed her a bag. "Can you get moving? I have some questions about your work at Weingart's."

"See? That didn't take long." I smiled at him.

"I need help understanding who the local players are in the wine business, who stood to gain from Andrew's death."

"All right but you know I'm new in town and don't know every winery owner. I do know a few, though."

"Yes, but you are the closest thing to a wine professional that we have who isn't necessarily a part of the local industry."

"Yes, but I really don't know enough about what I'm doing at that job. I do, however, know about wine."

"Come on, I need to go to the morgue."

"Oh, no, I need to go to work. I didn't sign up for this. I'm only participating in the wine part of this murder."

"You need to come. You can't sit in my truck; it's too hot outside anyway."

"But there are dead people in there."

"The medical examiner found some information that he thought might be interesting for Sanchez and me."

"That doesn't include me."

Frisco opened his Ford Explorer and waited for me to get in. "Look, Daisy, I didn't want this any more than you did, but here we are."

"I have a job I need to be at. How long is this going to take?"

"What time do you start work today?"

"That long, huh? Anyway, I'm curious to know if there will be people coming to the wine tasting room right after the murder. It's pretty grotesque if you ask me. I mean that's the last place I would want to be."

"And yet that's where you want to be."

"This really wasn't my idea. I do, however, expect to put down roots here. I'm going to need some money. I'm good at what I do."

Frisco pulled over in front of a modern white building. I could see Morgue written in black on a placard on the front. We made our way to the back where Frisco parked his truck, and I quickly opened the door and jumped out.

Entering the morgue, I smelled a heavy, sickly smell, and started to gag.

"Got no stomach for it, you can wait in the lobby. It doesn't matter to me."

He was maddening, but I was attracted to him in some perverse way. Whenever he spoke, he sounded like he was inside the chamber of a bass drum — deep, and very warm.

{ 23 }

"Wine ... the intellectual part of the meal."
ALEXANDER DUMAS

Entering the morgue, the coroner took one look at me and said, "The smell is something you get used to when you are around it often enough, but we carry the vapor-rub for those who aren't used to it."

The odor. I hoped my large, deer-in-the-headlights stare conveyed gratitude because I didn't want to open my mouth in case the peach jam made its way back up.

"Well, doctor, you said on the phone you had some information?" Frisco said.

"After looking into Andrew's death, I realized that following further analysis of his stomach contents he had been ingesting finely-ground glass. Even if he survived the stabbing, he wouldn't have survived much longer because the glass was tearing holes in his stomach lining."

"So basically someone had been murdering this guy for quite some time now," Frisco said.

"Yes. By the amount of glass content in Andrew's stomach I'd say he had been ingesting it for at least three weeks."

"How can you tell?"

"The glass is different colors and is at different stages of break-down by the acid in his stomach."

Running outside the room and hanging my head over a sink, I looked over my shoulder, "Can we go now?"

"Thanks, doctor. You gave us some interesting information." Frisco waved at me. "Come on, Daisy."

As we left, he said, "I think there was something else going down. Possibly sending a message to someone. But who? And who gave him glassware to eat?"

"What do you mean?"

"He was murdered by either a very impatient person, he knew something and was going to talk, or two different people were involved."

"So what you're saying is that he was eating glass, but wouldn't he know that he was eating glass?"

"That's what the doctor said. I think the murder of Andrew was an act of anger by someone he trusted. I think you should get a list of patrons and addresses from Mr. Weizner."

"Okay, I'll try," I said.

Turning to leave, I knew there would not be a next time for me in that place. Well, maybe when I was dead.

{ 24 }

"Wine brings to light the hidden secrets of the soul, gives being to our hopes, bids the coward flight, drives dull cares away, and teaches new meaning to the accomplishment of our wishes."

HORACE

Friday was a long day. I did double duty, working in the wine tasting room on site and then out in the fields. I drove home to Fresno to get away and get a good night's sleep, where I was greeted by Freeway. I got us dinner and collapsed in front of the television, but I didn't eat anything. There was too much on my mind.

I woke up early as if reluctant to start the day, and as the sun slowly entered the eastern sky, I wondered if that was a prelude of things to come. It was the weekend, and I decided it was time to make some changes in my life. I fed Freeway, got myself a cup of coffee, then we left in search of tranquility.

I drove through the foothills toward Oakhurst and by the same Tuscan villa I had seen on previous visits. It was still for sale. I wanted to see this land one more time and get my pal's approval. I wandered around the property for a while; it looked like it had been vacant for some years and was a bit run down.

As Freeway and I wandered around, I saw egrets on a nearby lake. They began their morning rituals, diving into the clear water, then floating above it. On the gusting wind, I occasionally heard their songs as they twisted and darted. I felt like I found Shangri-La. Looking at the beautiful land before me, the lake was a stunning aqua against the morning sky, the hill and mountains of Yosemite so stark in their wonder, I could scarcely believe the owners didn't fight harder to keep their home. There was a sense of peace that emanated from this place.

Maybe one day I'll buy it. Maybe. In the meantime, I gathered myself to drive back down to Weingart Winery to reality and the murder of Andrew.

I worked the entire day in the lab with Freeway by my side and was excited about a new grape cross blend I put together. The day was turning out okay after all.

The lease on my studio apartment was up at the end of the month. It was getting tiresome driving to Oakhurst almost every day, plus it really drained my gas tank and my pocketbook for lodging when I needed to stay the night in town like tonight. Thank God I had Freeway with me. I still had the cash hidden away, but I was saving that for my Tuscan villa.

I drove to town and rented a room back at the Chateau Inn. They accepted dogs as long as I paid a cleaning deposit so it worked out. I walked upstairs, key in hand, so I could shower and change for the evening. Freeway was exhausted and curled up in a corner on her bed. I headed downstairs for dinner at the Inn's fancy restaurant called the Ollalieberry House.

Looking around, I noticed that the restaurant, with its European country-estate atmosphere, was divided into three dining areas, each adorned with antique French provincial furnishings, magnificent tapestries, and original oil paintings, plus there was a stately terrace with a commanding view of the Sierra Nevada Mountains off each room.

Wandering around the downstairs area, I searched out the kitchen. I smelled steak, bread, and other assorted foods being prepared. A young girl washing dishes directed me to the cook. The aroma of the incredible food made my stomach growl. I hadn't eaten since the night before. I opened the kitchen door and spotted the chef.

"Hello," she said, looking up from the industrial stove.

"Everything smelled so good. I love the smell of fresh-baked bread; I hope I'm not bothering you."

"No, come in. Pull up a chair. Would you like some coffee while I cook up dinner for the guests?"

"I'd die for a cup right now. What are you cooking?" I asked while she handed me a hot steaming cup. "This is incredible. I can taste a hint of cinnamon."

The chef responded, "Thanks. I'm making pork tenderloins for dinner. Everything is handmade with local ingredients, even my jams and jellies. I doubt if you could find anything finer anywhere on this planet," she proudly said with a smile.

The owner of the inn walked in.

"Good evening. My name is Libby." She smiled and held out her hand.

Both the owner and the chef made me feel at home. I wasn't used to that. It was an effort on my part to sustain the niceties of a small town. I wondered if they knew Andrew or his wife? Maybe they could tell me about them.

"Daisy, what do you do?" Libby asked me.

"I work at Weingart."

"Oh, really! Did you hear what happened?"

"I was there. Did you know Andrew?" I asked quietly.

"Yes, I did; we went to the same church. I saw the announcement in *The Daily Tribunal* regarding Andrew's death. I called his wife and brought her dinner. What do you do at the winery?"

"I'm a viticulturist; I tend to the grapes. I also blend grapes together and make wine."

"There was a story in the paper of a couple who practiced law and came to Oakhurst as tourists," the chef interjected.

I'd thought she was going to talk more about the murder.

"Well, actually, they were on their way to Yosemite," Libby said.

"The couple bought a winery on Zimri Road."

I loved listening to the back and forth banter between the chef and Libby, but I was enthralled and impressed with the couple's guts. I mean for crying out loud, the guy was a lawyer. They had no experience, just a will to go after their dreams. If they could do it, I hoped I could. It was a matter of getting off the pot and committing myself. I had the education and the tenacity. It wasn't going to be easy doing this alone, though.

I certainly wanted to find out more about this article in the paper and see how this couple was doing. Libby told me they stayed at a Bed & Breakfast that overlooks the valley floor and northern Madera. They needed eight acres suitable for planting, most of which would end up being planted as pinot noir.

"How are they doing now?" I asked.

"They died. It was unfortunate, some type of an accident."

"You've got to be kidding me! What happened to their winery?"

"It was sold to Mr. Weizner."

{ 25 }

"And wine can of their wits the wise beguile, makes the sage frolic, and the serious smile."
ALEXANDER POPE

Getting to work was so much easier now that I was closer. During lunch I talked to one of the vintners in the field. He told me of a place near Coarsegold that was in need of repair and some TLC. It was the same Tuscan villa Freeway and I drove to the other day. It was perfect, and I still had all that money someone left me hidden in a safe deposit box. I decided to take a drive over to the villa and look around the place after work. I think I'll make a call to the man Katie introduced me to.

"Hi, Jack; this is Daisy. I'm going to drive to that villa across the street from you. When I'm done, if you have time, can I stop by?"

"Look forward to seeing you. I'll be finished feeding the horses by then."

It was almost sunset. I packed up my stuff and Freeway, and drove up the hill to look at the villa. It was a private estate situated in Mallard Meadows not far from Weingart Winery. It was a gated five-acre lot with an additional five-acre lot available next door. My new home — I was confident it was going to be mine — all 5500 square feet with four bedrooms and four baths. I walked in the front door and noticed the spectacular kitchen with wrap-around granite counters, copper hood and vent, halogen lighting, built-in refrigerator and freezer, commercial-grade dishwasher, and a commercial dual-fuel convection oven with six burners on the range and a pot filler faucet. The first floor had a floor-to-ceiling wine cellar with glass front. Walking outside, I spotted an old shed with its door unlocked. It seemed as if the previous owners left in a hurry. I checked it out. Inside was distillery equipment, barrels, and a tractor. My mind was scrambled. I mean I could buy this property and start my own winery. I walked through the grass and up the driveway and went back into the house.

I heard the front door open; it had to be a real estate agent checking on possibly listing the place. I knew I would be bombarded with questions like Why was I in this house if I didn't own it?

"How did you get in here?" the realtor said, a little annoyed.

"The door was open so I took a peek and then just kept going."

Seeing a potential buyer, she said, "The house hasn't been lived in for quite a while, and the kitchen needs updating. I can contact the owner of the property if you're interested in buying. Do you have any questions?"

"Not yet." I thought the kitchen looked great, but I wasn't a chef. As a matter of fact, cooking wasn't even in my wheelhouse.

"Good. Let me show you the rest of the home." Stepping through the kitchen, there was a family room with a unique travertine floor pattern. The floor-to-ceiling rock fireplace gave that wonderful cozy feeling. The realtor stepped aside and flourished her arm.

"Heading upstairs and to the left is the master bedroom with a sauna and hot tub. I'm sure you'll make good use of that."

I wasn't too sure about that, but it did have possibilities.

"A family lives in a mobile home on the property. They've tended the property for some years for the owner and are prepared to move if you choose to do something else with the property."

I loved real estate agents; they knew how to put you in the mind that the property was yours, and you could move right in or do whatever with it.

"Let me show you the barn."

"No, thank you. I've been here on several occasions and have already checked it out. All of the equipment comes with the place, correct?"

"Yes. I'm sorry; I didn't catch your name."

"Daisy Murphy."

"What a coincidence. There are daisy bushes right beside the front porch. Seems a bit serendipitous."

"Yes, I saw them, and they reminded me of my dad and a daisy bush we planted together when I was young."

I got a call on my cell from Jack while I was talking to the real estate agent. He told me he was free and that we could meet up as soon as I was finished. I was excited to tell him about my plan.

"I saw you talking to the agent. Are you really considering the property across the street from me, Daisy?"

"I am. I feel I belong here. I have some money saved and money I inherited," I lied.

"There are some things I've wanted to talk to you about but have been hesitant. I wanted to get to know you and you me. Would you like some coffee?"

"Yes, thank you."

I know it's been a very long time, but do you remember me from your childhood when you lived in Oakhurst?'

"You've always felt familiar to me. Haven't ever been able to place it, though. As you said, it's been a long time."

"Yeah, way too long. This might come to you as a shock, but..."

"You're my dad." It was a statement I hadn't thought of before, but there were too many coincidences for him to be anyone other than my father. I even remembered naming my first dog Prince.

"Well, that took a load off my shoulders. How do you feel about it?"

"I feel like I have a lot of questions to ask you, we have a lot of catching up to do, and that it's way too soon to call you Dad, but I can call you a friend."

"That's all I could ever hope for and more. So let's talk about that property across from me."

"Do you know who owns it?"

"Yes. I own it."

"Wait, what did you just say?" This was a bit too much to take in.

"I think it's about time you found out everything about us. That was your home, Daisy. Did you notice the daisy bushes near the front? We planted those just before your mom took you away."

"I still don't get that it's yours. Isn't it for sale?"

"It was until now. I hoped you'd want it when I first saw you with Katie and your interest in the community and the land. The property has always been in my family. When your mom left, I didn't know what to do. I kept it for the longest time but after so many years decided to sell it. After seeing you, I want you to have this home. I didn't know if you'd ever come when I was still alive," he said, smiling. "I didn't want to push you into anything."

Then something clicked. "Wait a minute. The money that showed up in my bank account. You put it there, didn't you?"

"I did. I wanted to help you get a fresh start in life with no concern of where you'd get your next meal. I always wanted you to be here, but I didn't know if that would happened in my lifetime. I inherited quite a bit from my folks so who better to share it with than you?"

"Thank you more than I can say! I love the home. Oh, my God, Jack. It's really part mine?"

"Whenever you say you're ready to take it over, it's yours. There's a lot of work to be done on the property. I've kept it up with the gardener's help but…"

"I have lots of things to digest right now, Jack. Can we meet again for dinner tomorrow night so I can formulate some questions that I've always wanted to ask my dad?"

Standing up from the table, I walked around and gave him a big bear hug and kissed his cheek. I felt a strong connection between us, something I'd missed for a long time. I grinned and headed to my truck and back to the Chateau Inn.

{ 26 }

*"A bottle of wine begs to be shared.
I have never met a miserly wine lover."*
CLIFTON FADIMAN

The next day I went back to the winery and walked out to the vineyards. Not much had changed; life in the field consisted of a water station and port-a-potties. The minimal basic needs were being met.

A helicopter fitted for crop dusting was spraying the neighboring field. José, who was a field hand and who had lived in the U.S. for 40 years, opened my eyes to the plight of the farm laborer who undergoes difficult working conditions that matches a crappy wage. On top of that, he told me that farm workers are poisoned by pesticides each year nationwide. Many cases weren't reported out of fear of losing the job, a beating, or being deported.

Farmworkers were relegated to the status of a disposable, impoverished labor system that resulted from the agribusiness system of food production. I felt for the farmer and the laborer, and I thought if the conditions were better, everyone would reap the benefit. Now they worried about being deported if ICE came calling. That certainly was held over their heads by an employer.

On my lunch break, I went to the Educational Employees Bank and transferred my bank account into Premier Community Bank because they seemed to cater to the local businessperson. Jimmy, who helped me set up my bank account before, was accommodating and knowledgeable about the area and familiar with my soon-to-be-home.

"If you don't know the area, I can point out different historical spots in Oakhurst, and we can have a great dinner at The Painted Lady," he said to me.

"I'm sorry, I have a lot on my plate right now, and although I would really enjoy that, I'll have to call you later," I said, blowing him off. It was nice of him to offer, but I had been warned about him by the cook at the inn, and I had my mind on other things and one man in particular whom I found intriguing.

I knew I shouldn't, but the next day I drove into town and splurged on furniture, including a king-sized bed made from lumber reclaimed from a Jim Beam distillery. It couldn't get much better than that. I purchased two comfy chairs that swiveled either to the desk or to the expansive windows that showcased the valley below. There was a large private balcony, a great place to enjoy the sweeping views of the valley's vineyards, orchards, and nightlife of nearby Fresno.

Every day in the late afternoon after work I walked over to take a look at my future home, staring at it and dreaming of all the possibilities. I gazed out at the Saddlebred across the way. Jack opened a gate from the round pen inside the corral.

"Hey, looking at your home?"

"Yes, and at all the possibilities," I said.

"Well, to my future neighbor," he said as he saluted me.

Jack watched me gaze at his horses galloping through the pasture.

"You liked looking at that grey the last time you were here with Katie. Do you ride?"

"No, Mom and I lived in the city, and there were no horses. I'd like to learn one day, though."

"How about we start you next week on that one? His name is Jeremy."

"You're kidding me! Really?"

"Absolutely. Come on up to the porch with me and have a cup of coffee. We can talk about riding lessons."

I took him up on his offer and continued to gaze out at the beautiful horse galloping around the pasture.

We walked to his home. I remembered doing this as a child, walking hand-in-hand with my dad when we crossed a street. It was a good memory. The smell of the place probably turned people off, but I loved the smell of horses, the green pastures, the hay, and yes, even the dung. There were also many dogs running loose that had been abandoned and the same with the cats. All found a home here.

Jack had a menagerie of other animals too — peacocks, guinea hens, and many more. Now some people might think that it was crazy finally feeling at home, but I did. For the first time in my life I felt safe.

I went to visit the horses and strays and took a riding lesson once or twice a week with Jack. Afterwards we sat on the veranda, watched the sunset, and drank a couple of beers. Jack was a lanky guy with dark hair and blue eyes very similar to my own. He had years of history to tell me of the area and of himself. I couldn't get enough information. The more I learned, the more I knew I belonged. I enjoyed our quiet evenings together, watching the horses running loose behind a white crossbar corral in the light green pasture. One evening, Jack told me about my grandparents and his hope of starting a winery one day.

"The dream died the day your mom ran out on me, taking you with her," he said looking at me. I saw the hurt that he still carried through the look in his eye. Not sure why he felt so much hurt from something that happened so long ago but I guessed we all carry our pains differently. I knew I still carried mine.

At the end of our conversation, I had this weird feeling that I only got on rare occasions. It was usually when I sat in front of my television, watching old movies. The feeling gave me comfort and security, something that I rarely experienced in my life. I thought, after I get back to our home at the Inn, Freeway and I need to watch an old movie like *Lassie*.

The next morning I got up and dressed for work. After a cup of coffee, I looked at my phone. There was a video; I wondered who'd sent it to me.

It was a recorded video of Katie. She was tied up, and someone was slapping her. Horrified, I replayed it again. I could see the terror in Katie's eyes. She was screaming for the person to stop. At the end of the video was a warning to me: *"Stay away from Andrew's murder and keep your mouth shut, or you'll be next. You would not want this to happen to you, would you?"*

{ 27 }

"When it comes to wine, I tell people to throw away the vintage charts and invest in a corkscrew. The best way to learn about wine is the drinking."
ALEXIS LICHINE

"Thanks for coming so quickly, Frisco. Let me get my phone; I think it's in my purse." I ran out of the living area of my room and went to the bedroom.

He was standing as tall and proud as a monument. He appeared to be shaped of granite and covered in tight, rippling muscles. And he smelled terrific. And why am I thinking this right now? Standing in front of him, I opened my bag and handed him my phone. "Press the message where there's a video."

"Who sent this?"

"I don't know. I'm terrified." Could this be from someone at the winery? I wondered. "That's Katie, my friend from college. At the end of last semester she called me, and it sounded like she was in trouble. I called the police, but they never found her. I should have kept looking. I should have retrieved her trunk like I promised Katie I would. Maybe there was a clue in it."

"What did she say?"

"She told me she saw something or overheard something. Before I could ask her more questions she hung up."

"Who did she work for?"

"Jack Mendez but he couldn't have had anything to do with what happened to Katie."

Frisco looked at me skeptically but said nothing.

"I'm late for my meeting, but I'll be back this evening and check on you."

I felt he was protective of me, and I liked it. I wanted to get up and stand beside him, wanted to touch him, but I had to get to work, and maybe this was a little too soon.

"It'll be okay, Daisy. I'll investigate this. Go to work, and I'll drive back home with you when your shift is done."

At the precinct, Frisco decided to talk to one of his friends about the local wineries. He felt that somehow the wine was the motive behind this case, but he wasn't sure how.

He called his friend Timothy who owned a beautiful bistro downtown and asked, "Timothy, have you been having any trouble with your orders or labels on wine bottles?"

"No, why?"

"Do you own any Weingart wines?"

"Only in my dreams I'm afraid; the wine he was about to put up for sale would retail at fifty grand a bottle. Connoisseurs the world over compete for an opportunity to attend his parties and buy a bottle of his wines."

As Frisco began to ask follow-up questions, Sanchez came jogging into the precinct. "Hey, is there any food around here?"

"I guess food is the only way to get you in here."

"Bite me, Frisco; there has been another murder."

Frisco's cell began to vibrate. He picked it up and listened. It was dispatch. "What, Burgess is dead? Where?" Frisco opened his car door and slid in. He was headed for a strip of land off of Highway 41.

"Sanchez, you coming?" he hollered as he started the engine.

"Where's that pretty date of yours, Frisco?" The ME asked while looking at Todd Burgess's body.

Ignoring him, Frisco took out his notepad and wrote down information and then took some pictures. "What's that in his hand?"

"An envelope. I was waiting for you before I pulled it out." He took it and held it out to Frisco.

"Man, that's a lot of cash. Was it a knife?"

"Yes. Look, there's a laceration into the abdomen." The medical examiner pulled the victim's jacket back.

"I can't verify what made the laceration until I get him back into my lab."

"Can you give us an idea?" Sanchez asked.

"Let me put it this way. As the energy is applied to the device in a more focused fashion, it requires less energy to cause significant injury. It was a very special knife, not typical."

"What the hell does that mean?" Frisco asked.

"Basically any organ that is penetrated with enough force can be injured and bleed. This fellow exsanguinated in a most gruesome way. It took him a couple of hours to die, but I'll know more later."

"Thanks, Doctor. Sanchez, let's get back to the precinct. I got some stuff I need to clear up."

"Care for a cup of coffee, Detective?" Marcie reached out and handed the detective a cup of five-hour mud.

"Thanks, Marcie. I needed this. Did you add something to it?" Frisco asked, not really paying attention.

"Why, yes, Frisco. Thank you for noticing. I laced it with cyanide," she said smiling.

Spitting the coffee back into the cup, Frisco looked at Marcie who had a shit-eating grin on her face.

He picked up a dry eraser pen and walked over to the suspect board. He started to draw a timeline of the crimes that had been committed in the last week. Who had a motive for the murders of Andrew Speck and Todd Burgess? What was the link? Who had the most to gain from their deaths? Why did Dave Brinker give an envelope full of money to Todd? Todd worked for Dave Brinker. Was it bribe money or money under the table for something that Todd did for Dave?

"Sanchez, can you look up Todd Burgess and see if he has any priors? And get a subpoena for his bank records while you're at it."

"Uhh sure. I'll get to that right after I finish my lunch."

What kind of mental state did the offender have to be able to commit this horrific crime? Was the perpetrator cunning and had something to gain?

Sounds a lot like Dave.

The culprit was organized, and several people met that criterion, including Weizner. The person was mobile, which described everyone at the party so that wasn't much of a lead. Was this the work of a serial killer? Frisco tossed these ideas over in his head.

He wrote everything he thought of on the board. It seemed to center around wine or the wine industry. Who were the main people in this town that were the most significant competitors in wine? Hans and Dave. But what had made one of them kill the sommelier?

Frisco walked away from the board and sat at his desk, picking up his cold coffee. It tasted like shit. He looked at his watch and saw it was late; he had promised Daisy he would escort her home. He went over to his chair, picked up his coat, and ran out the front door.

Daisy had got off early from work and decided to drive to the precinct to catch Frisco. "Is Frisco here?"

"Frisco?" Marcie yelled out. "Sorry, he was just here. I guess he's already left the building."

Looking around Frisco's desk, I noticed his notes of the crime on a whiteboard. Me? Did he put me on that board? I backed away and bumped into Frisco's desk and whipped around, knocking his coffee cup onto the floor. I found a file on Todd Burgess. So did Frisco believe these murders were random?

I didn't think so. They were linked somehow to each other. Marcie was working in the back room, and there was no one else around. I took a picture of the board and headed home. Frisco needed to explain why my name was on his list.

I waited for him to come for dinner. By ten o'clock he still hadn't shown. I leaned over and blew out the candles.

{ 28 }

"I have enjoyed great health at a great age because every day since I can remember, I have consumed a bottle of wine except when I have not felt well. Then I have consumed two bottles."

ATTRIBUTED TO THE BISHOP OF SEVILLE

At the vineyard, I saw my friend working. "Good morning, José; how're you doing?"

"If it weren't for this goddamn heat, everything would be fine. It's 110 degrees out here. Plus I had two of my employees pass out in the field. We were lucky enough to find them and get them into the hospital."

"Oh, my God. Are they okay?"

"Dehydrated. The hospital put them on fluids. I don't know how much more we can take. Farmworkers have few protections; they're at the mercy of those in charge of managing us all. We're not protected under the labor laws, which means less than minimum wage and hours guaranteed. My workers are not entitled to overtime pay or mandatory breaks for rest or meals. There are few labor protections for the children working on the farm either. We have no insurance, and the conditions are ridiculous to work in."

"I had no idea, José. Are the conditions here under Mr. Weizner good?"

"There are worse. There have been beatings, and I've seen women subjected to racial slurs, sometimes worse if they don't comply."

"Have you gone to the authorities regarding all of this?"

Looking at me as if I was a moron, José replied, "Daisy, I'm an undocumented worker. I'm not protected from retaliation by federal laws if I tried to organize a labor movement."

"I know that my job is primarily the viticulturist, but maybe I can talk to

Hans about putting up a tent and some misters. I'd like to see more up-to-date port-a-potties installed and plenty of drinking water available."

"I'd be grateful and so would all of the men and women."

"I'll go now and see what I can get done."

I got back into my truck and drove around to the tasting room but didn't see Hans's car. I had a hunch about some of the missing pieces on Frisco's board and parked where I usually worked.

There was a back entrance to the cellar where the wine barrels were stored. Hans had a key copied for me when I was first hired as an intern. Now it finally came in handy.

It was dark inside, and I was reminded of the fact that Hans was known for his discerning nose and his ability to identify wines in blind tastings. I wondered whether he might possess the skills of a mixer, the type of expert whom vineyards employ to achieve a precise blend of grapes. It was possible he concocted forgeries by mixing various wines and even a hint of port, as many forgers were known to do, in order to create a cocktail that tasted like it came from Andrew Jackson's own winery and put it under his own label, if he was lucky enough to own a bottle of Jackson's wine.

I looked around to see if there was a lab on the premises. I decided to go to where the crime had been committed. I approached, trying to keep as quiet as I possibly could. I saw a man crouching at the locked door, trying to pick it. I hid behind some wine barrels and watched as he opened the door.

A beam of light shot out from the flashlight that he held. Before he put it away I saw it was Frisco.

"Hey, Frisco. What are you doing here?"

Falling back against the door, I heard him say, "Shit," and then he lowered his voice, "Shh, I could ask you the same thing?"

"I work here." I shuddered, unwilling to believe the vibrant sensations he roused in my heart.

"Not down here, Daisy."

"I have more right here than you do."

"Okay, let's stop playing tit for tat. I'm down here on a hunch. I was wondering if Andrew knew something he shouldn't have and was killed for the information. I was taking another look at the crime scene. Now, why are you here?"

"The more time I spend with Hans, the more suspicious I become of him," I said.

"Why do you say that?"

"Just the other day Dave Brinker wanted to buy one of Weizner's new bottles of wine for fifty thousand dollars."

"That doesn't sound suspicious," Frisco said.

"It does if he turned him down. It was the wine he introduced at the party." I wish I had tied my tousled hair back in a braid; it was spilling over my shoulders and getting in my way.

"The one with the dead body near it?"

"Not that exact one but in one of the other barrels."

"Doesn't sound like Hans. I wonder why he turned down that kind of an offer?" Frisco said. "That's why I came here — to check the wine myself."

"Maybe it's counterfeit. Remember those missing labels?" Daisy said.

"What do you mean by counterfeit?"

"Think of it like perfume."

"You've got to be kidding me."

"No, I'm dead serious. In the malls there are perfume stores where you can buy a counterfeit Channel No. 5 or some other expensive perfume. The people behind the counter mix the different blends to make up a fake Channel. What if Hans or Dave were counterfeiting wines, and Andrew wanted a bigger take?" I said.

"I get it. Maybe Todd got wind of this fake wine, became partners with Andrew, and then they both wound up dead," Frisco said.

"I don't think Hans would have killed his sommelier at his party. I mean he was trying to get the attention of wineries around the world. His parties are lavish with a lot of famous people in attendance. Having a murdered employee near the wine you're about to introduce wouldn't be a good selling point," I said.

"I thought that as well; let's take a look."

"After you, since you know the place."

I headed into the lab ahead of Frisco and heard something move.

{ 29 }

*"The wine cup is the little silver well where truth,
if truth be told, doth dwell."*
SHAKESPEARE

Did you hear something moving? I asked quietly.

"No, be quiet for a moment and let me listen." After a moment he said, "Probably a mouse or some other creature."

I began to shake; I hated mice. Out of anxiety, I said in a hushed voice, "One of the things we need to consider is if Hans is a forger of wine."

"I heard rumors at the party that one of the wealthiest guests was screwed over. At first I thought he was just being petty, but now with everything that has happened, I'm not so sure." Frisco tilted his head. "Do you know if Hans has a laboratory where counterfeits could be made?"

"There's no lab here, but he has a large building in the back of his property. I've seen very few people go back there. It's kept locked day and night."

"How do you know that?" Frisco asked.

"I'm naturally curious about who I work for. By the way, how did you get in here?"

"I have certain tools that allow me to get into places."

"That's invasion of privacy and illegal, Detective."

"Yes, it is, Daisy, and so was what you did."

"Not as much as you." I wanted to stay with Frisco. I felt safe and protected, and I'd go with him to make sure he didn't trip walking out to the building.

"Tell me about the building."

"It's gated, and you need a code to get inside. It always has a man on the outside of the building. I've taken him water, cookies, and sandwiches before. He has, however, seen a truck deliver cases of empty bottles."

"I need to take a look at the building from the outside, get a lay of the land, and see if it is guarded at night as well."

"I thought I could help you with this."

"No, you're not going, Daisy; this could be dangerous, and I don't want you involved."

"I'm already involved, and if we don't go together, you know me well enough now to know that I will go it alone."

Scowling, Frisco reluctantly agreed on one condition. "Stay close to me and do what I say." I heard a sound again; it wasn't mice.

I grabbed Frisco and began to kiss him. He responded, pulling my tee shirt from my shoulder. Whether the tension I felt in him was because of the kiss or because someone was nearing us I wasn't sure. My heart soared the moment he touched me. I knew I should be frightened. Instead, I stood on my toes and circled my arms around his neck, eager to lean into him and give myself over to the amazing sensations of his kiss.

A flashlight directed at us showed our faces. I quickly pulled my tee shirt back up onto my shoulders. The intruder cleared his voice "What are you two doing down here?"

I peered over Frisco's shoulder and saw it was Hans. "Oh, my goodness, you frightened me," I said nervously, feeling like a kid caught with her hand in the cookie jar. "I wanted to show the detective some of your imported wine and port that you have collected throughout the years."

Frisco turned around, smiling at Hans. "Well, it was the one way to get Daisy alone. If you remember our first date didn't end well." He put his arm around me possessively.

Embarrassed, I wanted to slug Frisco, but I was grateful he followed through with an excuse for trespassing. Instead, I said, "Sorry, Hans. This won't happen again." The turbulent feelings I had at the same time were frightening and thrilling.

"At least not here it won't. I think my place would be better." Frisco smiled.

Hans gazed at us, not believing a word we said, but he laughed anyway. "Okay, kids, I get it. Daisy, I think you're supposed to be looking over the vines. Get going."

"So, Detective, how are things going on the investigation?" Hans asked.

"Slow but that's to be expected."

"I feel so badly about Andrew's family. He was a good man." Hans scrutinized the room.

"How long had Andrew been working for you?"

"We met in 2000 at the International Wine Championship. The IWC is held annually to pit English wines against wines from other countries. We hit it off. At the time, he was working for Dave Brinker. When I offered him a job with a substantial increase in his pay, he jumped ship."

"Do you think Dave had anything to do with Andrew's murder?"

"In this business Dave is an unforgiving man, and Andrew was always looking for any kind of action that would make him money."

"I think I'll go visit with Brinker in just a while, Hans. You've been very helpful. I do have one more question, though. Why would you need a sommelier? You know your wine and could do the job. They're not an enologist or a viticulturist, correct?"

"True but I needed someone who had a good nose for wine, good with the community, and who was good with customers."

"Interesting. I have no idea what you just said."

"How so may I ask?"

Ignoring his question, he said, "So someone with such skills could be employed for another reason."

There was a pause in the air, but Hans gave no reaction to the bait that Frisco threw out. Hans scratched his chin.

"What do you think he was involved in?"

"I'm not sure. I have a lot of theories simmering. Do you have any ideas?"

"If I were you, I'd go have a visit with Dave and get his input."

"Thanks, Hans, I'll do that."

"Anytime, Detective. I'm always here to help you and this community. Would you like me to go with you to see Dave?"

"No, that won't be necessary. Thanks again."

"By the way, how did you get into this area? It's always locked."

"I guess someone slipped up."

{ 30 }

"It takes a lot of beer to make a good wine."
LOU PRESTON

I went to the vineyard to check on the grapes. It was difficult concentrating because I kept thinking about Frisco, and that gave me chills. Who was I kidding? It would never be possible. He was a detective and my mom a missing murderer. I had to stop thinking about him and start thinking about my job. The harvesting of wine grapes was a crucial step in the process of wine making, and if I missed something, I could endanger the entire crop.

On my way back from the vineyards, I saw Frisco leaving and wondered again if Hans had anything to do with Andrew's murder. There were two types of wine counterfeiters: those who didn't tamper with what was inside the bottle and those who did. Because Hans had kept his Mission de Madonna Noire wine under wraps with Andrew, they would be the latter if they were forgers. Many forgers started with a genuine bottle of say a 1980 Petrus and merely replaced the label with one from 1982, an exceptionally coveted and expensive vintage. With a good scanner and a color printer, which Weizner and Brinker both had, labels were easy to replicate. I just didn't think Hans and Andrew did that; it was too easy to get caught because the cork was marked with the year. Forgers scratched away the last digit expecting the people they sold to not to notice or say anything. I thought Hans was much more aggressive. If he stole wine, then he had to have a much broader plan. That building on the other side of the property was critical to proving my theory.

Catching up to Frisco on his way back to his truck, I asked, "Can we meet later tonight and look inside the building together?"

"I'm taking Savannah out for dinner and a movie."

"Of course, but after that long kiss you gave me …" His crystal blue gaze stole my breath away.

"I didn't kiss you; you kissed me."

"But you enjoyed it." I knew he felt the same powerful connection. My hands reached out and rested on his chest, splayed across his heart. I tried not to show my disappointment at its calm and steady beat. Mine were wild and pounding in my ears.

{ 31 }

"Wine makes every meal an occasion, every table more elegant, every day more civilized."
ANDRE SIMON

It was the end of the day for me, and I was about to embark on my favorite past time, walking over to the home that one day would be mine. Just before I opened the door to leave, Hans approached me.

"Daisy, can I speak to you before you go?"

"Sure, Hans. What can I help you with?"

"I'm devastated about Andrew. You will inform me if Frisco finds out who the murderer is or anything that will help me with the media. I just don't understand how such a thing could happen. I know this sounds self-serving, but why on earth would someone do such an act at my place of business?"

"Sure, Hans; I'll let you know if I learn anything new."

"Do you think it was a crime of passion?" Hans asked.

"Your guess is as good as mine."

"Please, Daisy, help me get ahead of this. The local newspaper carried an unflattering report about me and the wine I was promoting the night that Andrew was murdered."

"I'm sorry to hear that. I know this means a lot to you. Everything was going so well, and the party was a hit. The people, the community … everyone loved the wine you served, and everyone couldn't wait to try your new one. Until of course, Andrew showed up dead. I do have a question for you, though, Hans. Why did you turn down Mr. Brinker's offer to buy a bottle of your new vintage?"

"I wasn't quite ready to sell it yet. I wanted to make sure we had many buyers who enjoyed it. I could even raise the price. And thank you, Daisy. I knew I could count on you," he said tersely.

"Have you given any thought to my suggestions for the workers? Their housing, the amount they're charged for water, the lack of a facility to use on their breaks, breaks they don't get time to take. I'm concerned about their working conditions."

"Of course, they have breaks, but my supervisor is very strict. These people are always fooling about and just lie around trying to collect money for work not completed. They also call in sick all the time."

"Maybe if there were a cooling station under a tent, some decent port-a-potties, and a couple of chairs for them to take a rest on, they wouldn't become so ill. I've been out there, Hans, and I think a few things need to be changed."

"I'll talk to the supervisor and make sure my farm workers get the attention they deserve. I think you need to start calling me Mr. Weizner. It's more appropriate considering you work for me. Is that clear?"

"Crystal."

{ 32 }

"I serve your Beaune to my friends, but your Volnay I keep for myself."
VOLTAIRE

Frisco arrived earlier than usual at the precinct, coffee cup in hand. "Someone's dead at the Brinker's home, Frisco," Marcie said.

"Who?"

"The local police didn't say, but they're asking for a detective so I believe it's another murder."

"Will Sanchez be there?" He didn't even get a sip of coffee and now he had to leave. He was not in a good mood.

"He will be."

Picking up his jacket off the back of his chair, Frisco moved quickly toward the door. "See you later."

Pulling up to the Brinker's home, Frisco saw that Sanchez was already there, his window down. He handed the tablet to Frisco.

Frisco scrolled through the images of the crime scene. The violence had escalated, and Dave Brinker was the unfortunate recipient.

Now they had three victims, and somehow these murders were related. How he didn't know, but he didn't believe in coincidence, and they were too close not to be connected.

"Who was the first officer on the scene?" Sanchez asked.

The young police officer answered, "Me. I was closest."

Frisco left Sanchez and after searching the perimeter of the estate, walked in the front door. He put his white booties on.

"Doc, do you know how and when he died?" Frisco asked the ME.

"I'm checking his liver mortise, and it looks like between one and four this morning, Frisco. I'll know more after the autopsy."

"There is vomit all over him and the house, he had a bloody stool, and a bluish tinge around his lips. Look here, Sanchez," the ME said, pointing to the dead man's lips. "Oh, and no trauma to the body. He could have been poisoned."

"What kind of poison could do that?"

"Ricin. I know that it is one way of causing this." He pointed around the room and then to the body.

"Well, that narrows things down a bit, doesn't it? Ricin can't be that easy to get."

"Actually, Ricin comes from the Castor plant. A single seed could kill."

"Oh, great. Well, let me know what you find out."

As Frisco and Sanchez headed out the front door of the house, Frisco spotted Daisy standing outside the police perimeter.

"What are you doing here?" Frisco asked.

"I was coming from Jack's on my way to work. I saw all the police cars in front of Dave's so I stopped. What happened?"

"I think you need to leave now."

"I saw Dave just last night at Timothy's restaurant in town. This is so sad," I murmured.

I watched as the coroner lifted Dave's body onto the gurney with the help of his assistant.

"Sanchez, let's go to Timothy's restaurant and talk to him," Frisco exclaimed. "I think you need to get to work or something, Daisy."

"Fine."

"I'll see you tomorrow night if you'd like to go out."

Looking up at Frisco, I grinned, hopped into my truck, and slowly drove away. I guess he didn't forget about our kiss after all.

{ 33 }

*"Wine is at the head of all medicines;
where wine is lacking, drugs are necessary."*
BABYLONIAN TALMUD: BABA BATHRA

It was pitch black, except for the large LED street lamps that gave the sun a run for its money so blending in with the night sky was pretty much out of the question. I searched the grounds for Frisco to meet up for our date. It was hard to believe that I couldn't find him with Fifteen Shades of Suns lighting up the surrounding area of the mysterious wine lab.

Tiptoeing around the perimeter of the lighted structure and trying not to alert the night guard, I tripped over a bush. Before I hit the ground, Frisco whispered, "Not only are you as visible as a neon sign, but everything about you screams Look at me, everyone. I'm trying to sneak around the premises."

"I'm sorry. I wasn't trained in the art of breaking and entering. Was that a class the precinct offered because I think I was getting my nails done at the time?" I wanted to laugh when I looked at his face so full of concentration, but I was too afraid of getting caught and losing my job. He motioned for me to follow him to the back of the lab. I noticed that either someone forgot to shut a window or Frisco had jimmied it open. He cupped his hands for me to put my foot in his palms so that I could get inside.

Slowly I shimmied my way in, wiggling through the tight space as quietly as I could and feeling around for something to grab onto so I could pull my way through and not land flat on my face. My fingers touched a metal coat rack that was attached to the window. I grabbed it and pulled myself through and onto a bench without breaking anything.

Frisco hoisted himself through the window effortlessly and landed softly on the bench just like a cat. Color me impressed.

We worked silently together, looking for evidence. I saw a ledger that I assumed was used to record the chemical properties for dissecting the wine. I wondered if Dave, Todd, or Andrew knew about this lab and if what I suspected was true about Hans's counterfeiting operation. If so, had they been killed because of it? I looked over to Frisco as he pulled a plastic bag out of his coat pocket to capture a sample of wine to submit to the police laboratory for analysis. I hoped that the scientists could reconstruct the experiments. Although there were hundreds of cases of wine from France, there were no beakers, necessities for counterfeiting.

Outside and back at our respective vehicles, Frisco said, "Unless the lab finds something this was a bust."

"I'm sure something will turn up," I answered more optimistically than I felt. He left me as he had an early morning press briefing on the investigation he told me. People in this small mountain community were becoming frightened, and the chief and the mayor wanted the killer caught sooner rather than later. So did I!

Leaving the lab and distancing myself away from Frisco, I looked over at the Manzanita plants that covered the hills and valleys of Yosemite. I loved my new home, but there did seem to be quite a lot of murders in a short amount of time.

{ 34 }

"In the order of names, these are the hardest to control: wine, women, and song."
FRANKLIN P. ADAMS

I felt we were getting closer to identifying whoever had murdered three people. Frisco may now have a better idea because of the evidence collected, but I wasn't privy to that. I had a sudden craving to know more about Hans.

What kind of man would attract so many followers — the rich, the famous, the gullible, a con man? More to the point, was I being pulled into becoming one of his followers, a cult drooling over every glance, praise, and attention that he gave me. I wondered again if there was more to Hans than merely an owner of rare wines.

I arrived at my room with Freeway at two in the morning and turned on the light. I knew immediately that someone had been inside. Everything was askew, not enough for most people to notice but enough that things I placed a certain way like the magazines on the table were out of order. I threw my jacket onto the bed and noticed there was a plate of cheese and crackers with a note next to it.

"Daisy, remember Inglewood. I haven't forgotten."

I backed away, wanting to run out of the room. I couldn't breathe. I felt cold all over, and I was terrified that I was going to die. Then I was horror-stricken. Maybe the intruder was still in my room?

I heard someone knocking on the door. I couldn't move, but I let out a scream. Freeway started barking and growling, and the room around me began to fade.

I had to hide the note before anyone else saw it. I reached out and grabbed it.

"Just keep breathing, Daisy," I heard a familiar voice say. "An ambulance is on its way. You're going to be fine. Just keep breathing," Frisco said.

{ 35 }

"Wine is a living liquid containing no preservatives. Its life cycle comprises youth, maturity, old age, and death. When not treated with reasonable respect, it will sicken and die."

JULIA CHILD

The doctor said it was a panic attack and gave me a prescription," I said to Frisco as we left the hospital grounds.

"I'm sure this has been very traumatic for you, Daisy. Are you sure you don't want me to walk you up to your room?"

"No, I'm fine now and thanks for being there for me." Frisco dropped me off to check on Freeway before going to work. Putting my key into the lock, I glanced up and saw someone out of the corner of my eye before entering. There was no clear-cut image of the person. The face was obscured by the sun coming through the window in the hallway of the hotel. Was this the person who left the message in my room? The individual looked oddly familiar, though, but I couldn't pull the image up in my mind. I only had a fuzzy recollection of seeing him or her before. I whistled for my dog. She came out of the bathroom and jumped into my arms. Maybe I was becoming paranoid. I couldn't understand what was going on. Was I losing my mind? Was I becoming my mother's daughter?

I picked Freeway up and held her tightly to my chest as I raced down the stairs to my truck. I was shaken. I pulled to the side of the road to calm myself. I rummaged through my purse for my cell phone and called Frisco and told him what I saw back at the Inn. This nightmare began with Andrew's death. Could all of this just be a coincidence?

As soon as I arrived at the winery, I made my way to the orchard to escape the intensity of the last few days. I figured the one place I could escape my thoughts would be out there. It was quiet and serene, feelings I tried to obtain on my own but was failing miserably.

I walked back to the wine cellar where it was too dark to see and switched on the floodlights.

"What?" someone yelled.

"Is anyone down here?" I asked. I saw a head peep around one of the barrels.

"Good morning, Charlotte." Hans's assistant looked up at me. "I haven't seen much of you since the party."

"That was a ghastly affair, Daisy. I have avoided coming down here since then."

"But why are you down here in the dark?"

"I have a flashlight," she said as if that answered the question.

"Do you remember seeing anyone who stood out at the party to you that maybe didn't belong, or maybe they belonged but just not at the party?"

"I've already gone over this with the police," Charlotte said, wringing her hands nervously. "But wait. I did see a woman in a black trench coat. Odd for this time of year, don't you think?"

"I do remember seeing someone in a trench coat who looked familiar, but I thought it was just someone I saw in the tasting room. I wondered who she was."

"I saw her in the corner to the side of the barrels; she did seem out of place."

"Do you think you could recognize her if you saw her again? Maybe something will jog your memory or both of ours if we talk together. I remember when I first started my internship, you said something that stuck with me. 'To catch a thief, you have to be a thief.' What did you mean by that?" I asked tersely.

"I don't have a clue to what you're talking about, Daisy," she retorted. "Look, if it's all the same to you, mind your own business. The Madera police department is working on this case. You're just a vintner. Do the job you're paid to do."

I felt the heat rise to my face. "I'm sorry if I offended you." Actually, I really wasn't sorry about anything. If she had something to do with the murders, why would I care if I offended her?

"These murders started happening when you arrived. I'm not saying you're a murderer, but it seems pretty coincidental, don't you think? Now let it go!"

"I've been here a year, but you're upset. I understand and would think the same in your place, but I was hoping you could remember if there was anyone else who seemed out of place that evening? Remember, I was up here with you guys doing a mystery taste testing. I'm scared, Charlotte! Someone just left a note in my room where I'm staying. I don't want to be the next victim in whatever is going on here."

"I'm sorry, Daisy, but it has nothing to do with me. I'm going back upstairs. Lock the door when you come back up."

This was my last chance to know if she had anything to do with what was going on. "Charlotte, if you know something, I can help."

"Yeah? I don't think so." She took a tissue out of her purse to dab at her eyes. She turned back around to face me. "I have no idea what you're talking about, Daisy." She fled back up the stairs, not looking back but stopping just at the top landing.

Sounded like I hit a nerve. "Charlotte, although I haven't lived a long life, one thing I have learned is that the truth usually comes out. If another murder takes place and you know something, you need to tell someone. Tell Frisco or anyone before it's too late. This person may kill again, and if you know something and don't say anything, you are a part of the murder. You'll be culpable."

She glared at me and then turned and walked away.

{ 36 }

"The two professions {filmmaking and wine making} are almost the same. Each depends on source material and takes a lot of time to perfect.
The big difference is that today's wine makers still worry about quality."

FILMMAKER AND WINE MAKER; FRANCIS FORD COPPOLA

I felt a little stronger after a good night's rest. I took a long shower, enjoying the hot rush of water that poured over my body. It seemed to loosen every knot I had tied up in my neck. Drying off, I put on my comfy old jeans and shirt. I opened the slider door and sat down, sipping a cup of coffee and patting Freeway.

I picked up the journal where I wrote all my thoughts down every day since I first enrolled at CSUF. I read back about the wine party and sat up, alert at the passage I had written.

I noticed that at the beginning of the party I saw Charlotte speaking with the guests, and when Andrew arrived, she said something to him just before he went to the cellar. Maybe chastising him for being late. That was when Frisco drove up in his truck. After the wine tasting game, we all went down to the cellar, including Dave. Andrew had already gone down. I looked for Charlotte but couldn't find her.

I looked up and wondered how I could have missed that.

After Andrew, Todd had been murdered. Frisco mentioned that he saw Todd walk off; maybe he gained something, won the argument, I didn't know. I didn't even think Frisco knew for sure, but within days Todd turned up knifed to death. So Andrew and Todd were definitely out of the running for trying to scare me. But were those two murders connected in any way? Were they wine counterfeiters? Was Dave a part of this? I really wished Frisco would share some of his information on the case with me, but he told me that I was on a need-to-know basis.

I felt a chill go up my spine. Someone was watching me; I sensed it. I gazed out at the surrounding trees. Freeway started barking.

{ 37 }

"Hardly did it appear,
than from my mouth it passed into my heart."
ABBE DE CHALILIER, 1715, UPON FIRST TASTING CHAMPAGNE

In the distance I saw someone running away. I ran down the stairs with Freeway in the direction of the "peeping Tom," then picked up my cell to take a picture, but that someone stopped suddenly and glared at me. I walked back to my room and copied off a print to give to Frisco later.

I drove with Freeway to the vineyard in a sort of fog. Who could it be? Why was that person watching me?

I saw José as I drove up. He was speaking with the foreman of the winery. The conversation looked heated so I got out of my car to see what was going on.

"Don't push me!" José demanded.

"You need to get off the property. You've been fired," the foreman said, sticking his index finger into José's chest.

José slammed his fist into the foreman's jaw. "You fuck; get out of here."

"Come on, José! Let's go before the cops come," I screamed.

José glanced at me but pushed me aside and made another charge at the foreman. The foreman grabbed him around the neck with his forearm and beat him in the head. Blood was flying as the two men fell to the ground, grappling with one another. I heard sirens approaching.

Screeching to a stop, the cops jumped out of their cars with their guns drawn. Hans walked out of the office. "This man," he said pointing to José, "started the fight. I fired him, and he needs to get off my property."

"Wait, I saw the foreman push José first."

"Stay out of it, Daisy," Mr. Weizner said.

"But it's the truth." I looked at the foreman as he was wiping the blood from his nose.

The cops grabbed José and handcuffed him, throwing him into the back of their squad car.

"José, I'm so sorry." I couldn't believe this was happening.

Daisy, go to my office," Hans ordered.

"Why? This isn't right."

"I said go to my office now."

I turned in the direction of Hans's office and waited for his arrival with Charlotte.

"Daisy, why do you always butt in where you don't belong?" Charlotte asked.

I was so angry I said nothing to her. "I've told you before to keep out of everyone's business."

Hans slammed the door. "Daisy, get your stuff and leave."

"What? You're firing me, too?"

"Yes, you're fired. This had nothing to do with you. The foreman was doing his job and what I told him to do."

"You told him to beat up José? Why?"

"Leave."

I left Hans's office and picked up my belongings. Some of the workers waved and looked sadly at me.

I waved back and drove up the hill to the Inn. I called Frisco at the precinct to tell him about the peeping Tom and the picture I took.

"I'll call you later," he said. He was busy going through the evidence that they collected from Dave's murder.

"Before you go I need to tell you that I'm heading to Madera to pick up José."

"I heard all about it. How are you going to pay for his bail?"

"I've got it handled, Frisco."

"What about your job? You certainly don't want to piss off Hans."

"Too late, Frisco. Not only did I piss him off, but I got fired in the process."

"Jeez, I'm sorry, Daisy. What are you going to do?"

"I have a plan in place; it's just happening sooner than I expected. I've got to believe that everything happens for a reason." God, let it be so.

"Good luck. I'll see you tonight at The Lobster House around 7:00. Does that work for you?"

"I'm out of a job. Anytime would work," I said with a laugh.

Leaving the Inn, I had no idea what it would take to get José out of jail, but whatever it was I was prepared to do it. Freeway jumped into the back seat, and we drove down Highway 41 to the Madera Sheriff's office.

"Can I help you?" an officer asked from behind his desk.

"Yes, please. I'm here to bail out José Gonzalez. He was brought in this morning." I was shaking in my boots, and the officer kept looking at me with a puzzled expression.

"Are you his lawyer?"

"No, sir, just a friend. What do I need to do?"

The officer went to his computer and told me how much money I needed to put up bail. He walked to the filing cabinet and pulled out José's record. "Do you need a bail bondsman?"

"No, sir. Will you accept a check?"

"We need a cashier's check."

"Can you tell me where the nearest Premier Community Bank is?" Being here made me feel as if the next time I came back in, they would have discovered my past and arrest me.

"There's one around the corner. When you get back with the check, we'll get him ready to go with you."

"Fine, thank you, sir," I said, turning toward the exit and making a quick getaway.

Since the night my mother blew a hole through Mike's head I always hated speaking with cops because they reminded me of what I'd left behind. Frisco, however, was an exception.

I made a call, found out what it would take, and picked up the check. I returned, and a few hours later José was released. I took him back to Oakhurst where he retrieved his belongings from the winery. We picked up his wife and kids on the way to my new home, where he agreed to live and work for me. None of us had much choice. I was moving in quicker than I'd thought. I hadn't done much with the cottages on the premises, but it was a place for José and his family to live.

"Thank you, Daisy. I don't know what to say. I hated being in that jail."

"First, your thank you is perfectly sufficient. Second, how did you get that black eye?"

"Some of the men in the tank weren't too happy to make my acquaintance."

"Shit, I'm so sorry I couldn't get you out sooner. However, I had the power turned on in the cabins. I'm out of a job as well so I guess it's up to you, me, and Freeway to get this winery back into business."

"Is this a permanent job offer?"

"Yes, it is, if you'll take it."

"It's a lot of work, Daisy. I'm not sure if I can do this."

"I think we can, and I believe we will. Do you have a couple of men who could start work tomorrow setting up the water system for the vines? When we complete that, we can start on the barn and cottages and get ready to plant the vines."

"I know several men if you don't mind poaching them from Mr. Weizner," he said cautiously.

"I don't have a problem at all. There are a few cottages for them and their families. They're not in the best condition, but they can fix them up instead of paying rent for the first year. I'll have beds, refrigerators, sofas, and other necessities delivered by next week. There's also a caretaker already living on the premises so I can tap him for some extra help."

"Let me take my wife and our belongings to our home, and I'll meet you out in the field. Do you have an idea what you want to plant?"

"I've been planning this since I graduated so, yes, I know exactly what I want."

"Is this house and land all yours?"

"According to my dad, he's owned it for quite a while. Jack just recently signed a quick claim deed over to me. I was staying on with Mr. Weizner, trying to learn a few more things, but you have to be prepared for life's changes."

"I hope it's for the better for us all," José said with more confidence than he had before.

"I think it's up to us to make sure it is."

I left José and his wife Ruby to unpack, and I walked Freeway out to my truck. I saw Jack coming out to feed his horses. He waved at me and yelled, "Hello, neighbor! Finally decided to move in?"

I waved back and gave him thumbs up, then I retrieved my journal in which I'd been writing my plans for a winery and scratched out information on the murders. I walked up the stairs into the villa, deciding to look on the Internet for pictures of the Weizner family and for Hans in particular. He had to be the "black sheep" of his family or maybe a cousin?

I was working on my list of names of the Weizner family when Jack popped over. "Hi, Jack. Quick question. You were at Hans's party when Andrew was killed, right?"

"Yes, I was a guest. I don't usually attend his events, but I was interested in what he was up to."

"Why?"

"When Katie worked for me, she'd noticed some suspicious activity going on. She was dating one of the men who worked at the winery. One night she snuck into the lab in the back and tried to smuggle a beaker of liquid out. Someone came into the lab and caught her. She ran out and dropped the beaker."

"That was gutsy of her and maybe why she's missing. Do you think that Mr. Weizner had something to do with her disappearance?"

"Quite possibly. I didn't see her after that evening," he said, chagrined.

"One last question. Were you with someone in a trench coat?"

"Yes, a lady friend who owns an antique store in town."

"You're kidding me."

"She'd like to talk with you, Daisy. She remembers you when you were a little girl. Maybe she'll sell you a few things for your home at a discount."

"Do you two have something going on?"

"I don't think I'll answer that question," he grinned. "Go see her."

"Only because you're asking. And, of course, a discount would be great."

{ 38 }

"She gets to keep the chalet and the Rolls. I want the Montrachet."

ANONYMOUS

Charlotte, hello. This is Daisy. I need you to send my final paycheck to the Château and to ask you again if you remember anything about that evening when Andrew was murdered."

"What, ahh, no. I have said that a million times, Daisy. You shouldn't be calling here."

"Charlotte, there are three dead people you knew and were friends with. I think you know something." Once I started I wasn't about to hold back. I heard her take a big breath. When she spoke, grief and the release of shame trembled in her voice. "You're right, Daisy. They were friends of mine, and I never expected this to happen."

"I know, Charlotte."

"I met Todd at a party several years ago when he picked up some wine to take to Dave. Todd and I were more than just friends; he could make anyone love him. He was a free spirit who happened to get in way over his head with some terrible people."

I didn't say a thing; I could only imagine what it was like to finally give up what she was holding inside. I kept silent, waiting. I wanted to let her reach that point all on her own.

"Todd and I were very good friends as well. Do you have someone special in your life, Daisy?" Charlotte giggled.

"Not yet," I told her a little perplexed.

"It's hard to believe that someone could murder someone like that. I begged Todd to take us away before it was too late. I had already packed all of our belongings the night before the party. We had to get away."

I wondered why she felt they had to leave before it was too late.

"Andrew was greedy. I tried to overlook that one bad trait, but it got the best of him. I'm so very sad that he died."

Give me his name, the person who killed him, I begged silently.

"Hans and Andrew stole a bottle of rare wine years ago when they were in Europe. They secreted it out of the country. Then Andrew got wasted and told Todd. The two schemed together to soak the labels off of the expensive counterfeit wine of Hans, then traded them out for Dave's less expensive bottles that Todd had complete control over. Dave's sales of wine sky-rocketed, and he had no clue. Todd was mesmerized by all of the money that was rolling in. He had no control. It was like he was an addict." She began to cry.

"But did Hans kill Andrew, Dave, or Todd?"

"No, of course not."

"So Hans's only crime was that he's a thief of the original bottle of Mission de Madonna Noire wine and the counterfeiting of it and renamed it Madonna Maria Noire wine?"

"Yes."

"Then who's the killer, Charlotte?"

{ 39 }

"Wine makes a man more pleasing to himself;
I did not say to others."
SAMUEL JOHNSON, APRIL 28, 1778

I began thinking of all the possibilities and connections running through my mind. Things were starting to piece together. Hans and Andrew were the original counterfeit thieves. Todd and Andrew stole the fake bottles of wine from Hans and put Dave's wine label on them. Dave was an innocent. But who killed everyone? Could Charlotte be wrong, or was she lying?

Charlotte needed to leave the estate immediately. If Hans was the murderer and he had motive, then she could be in grave danger. I had seen for myself Hans's anger with the farm workers.

I had to clean up for my date with Frisco. I checked back with José to make sure he was doing okay and was ready to start work tomorrow.

I sported a navy blue dress with matching sandals, added some make-up, and tied my hair back. Strolling into the restaurant, I saw Frisco glance at me.

"You look amazing!" he said.

The heat began rising to my cheeks, and my heart was beating like a hammer strike against my chest.

Frisco stood up and pulled out my chair. "I've ordered some champagne; I think I've had enough wine." The air felt charged between us when he gently caressed my cheek.

"Thank you. Yes, there's so much that has happened." I told Frisco about my talk with Charlotte. "Daisy, it seems Charlotte is in this whole thing as well. It might be difficult to prove Hans stole wine, but it certainly gives him motivation for killing Todd, Dave, and Andrew."

"So Mr. Weizner can't be prosecuted for stealing wine in France but what about counterfeiting and the murders?"

"There's no direct link to Hans, Daisy."

Frisco covered my hand with his. The air in the restaurant became heavy with the weight of possibilities.

"Why don't you come home with me after dinner? I'll show you around, and we can go over the evidence together. I'm sure you've done a lot of thinking on this," Daisy said.

"You've bought a home?"

"It's a long story, but, yes, and I'd like you to see it tonight."

"I could order a bottle of wine and dessert to take with us as a house-warming gift."

"That sounds like fun. Or we could skip buying dessert and get some at my house." I smiled at him.

"Check," Frisco called out. He regarded me with a wickedly appealing arch of his eyebrow.

Frisco followed me back to my villa, and then held my hand as I walked him around the estate, showing him the barn, my future wine tasting room, and where I would be planting new vines.

"Next time I come I'll bring you a bottle of champagne to celebrate." I liked that thought.

Strolling into the kitchen, I reluctantly let go of his hand and pulled dessert out of the fridge. Then I started a pot of coffee for us.

"I've been thinking," Frisco said.

"About?"

"Charlotte could have killed the men. But what would her motivation be? It seems Hans is more likely to have killed them. We have to keep this to ourselves until we have something substantial."

I smiled at the thought "Okay, let's eat. Dessert should never go to waste."

"Never."

{ 40 }

*"In victory you deserve champagne;
in defeat, you need it."*
KEVIN ZRALY

Charlotte Simmons called me and told me she had been fired by Hans. I invited her to meet me at the villa.

"Hans fired you? He's a dangerous man, Charlotte, and I think you being there is unhealthy. What I'm asking is would you like to be my assistant? You were invaluable at the winery."

"Daisy, I can't believe you're offering me a job after all that I put you through and what I've done," she said.

"We all make mistakes," I said, thinking about my own past. "I need someone who knows the business. I'm not offering you anything that someone else would not offer you. I'm just doing it first."

"You can count on me," she said with a smile. At forty-five, she had more experience and camaraderie with older clientele than I did. It was a good trait to have.

I brought José into the discussion, and we laid out the plans for building "The Grey Stallion Winery."

Jack left the grapevines untended so they grew along the ground, up trees, onto anything that was in their way. I decided that José would hire five men to have them trimmed and trussed. If he could get the help away from Hans, all the better.

Tomorrow they would begin to prune the old vines and build trellises. I shared my vision of the vineyard and how I'd develop the grapes. The dry farming method was a system in which we'd stave the vines of the luxuries of life to get the most out of the grapes. Luxuries like water tended to make the vines lazy, preventing them from growing to their full potential.

José left to hire laborers, offering them medical and dental insurance, good pay, and a home right here at The Grey Stallion Winery. He also went to a wholesale lumberyard and picked up the things we needed to get the men working in the next month. It would be a challenge.

Seeing Charlotte, I asked, "Where would you like your office? The heat is on in the future Tasting Room, and it seems like a comfortable place." I walked her over and let her take her time touching, looking, and basically feeling comfortable with her new working environment.

With a sigh, she looked at me and pointed to the office behind the bar. "I think this would be suitable. I can keep tabs on the wine, there is great lighting, my computer can go toward the back wall, and I can also keep an eye on the hostess, the customers, and the laborers outside."

Charlotte's cell phone rang. "I'm sorry, Daisy. I've got to go on an errand. I'll be right back."

"Wait, we've just started." I shook my head.

"Sorry. It's important."

After Charlotte's departure, I received a phone call from Frisco asking me to come to the precinct to help him go over some new information.

"We just received an anonymous tip regarding Charlotte. Don't get too close to her, Daisy. She's not exactly what she seems. You could be next on her list."

{ 41 }

"A man will be eloquent if you give him good wine."
RALPH WALDO EMERSON

Taking Freeway to the police station to meet up with Frisco got me a look of disapproval from Marcie at the front counter. "Daisy, dogs aren't allowed in here."

"She's been here before. I'm sorry. That came out a little too sharp. She isn't feeling well so I just need to keep an eye on her."

"Hold on, let me ask them," Marcie said begrudgingly. "Okay, you can go in," she said after hanging up the phone.

"Thank you for asking, Marcie. Wait a minute, you said them."

"The District Attorney and Frisco are in the office waiting for you. And now Freeway."

"What's going on?"

"I'm not privy to that information. Go walk yourself down the hall and find out."

"Thanks." I didn't like going into a closed-door meeting and being the only one out of the loop.

I walked into a cheerless room where the DA with steely blue eyes fixed his sight directly on my face.

"Daisy, this is District Attorney Charles Connor," Frisco said. I reached out my hand to shake his.

"Frisco tells me that you believe the three murders were done by Hans Weizner."

That hit me like a ton of bricks. I looked at Frisco. "I'm not sure all three were committed by him. I'm not even sure he did one. I know he's a thief and a counterfeiter of wine. There's a lot of money involved so yes, he could be a murderer, but I don't have proof."

I told the District Attorney about Mr. Weizner's connections to all three men and his involvement in the theft of the wine. I believed Dave, Andrew, and Todd stole the manufactured fake wine, and on my phone I had pictures of Hans's temperature-controlled lab with wine labels. I shared my belief that in order to sell his wine he could not be a member of the Weizner family because the real Weizner family had a solid reputation and connections. I brought out paperwork I got off the Internet about the Weizner family with family pictures and no mention of Hans.

"Why wouldn't one of these people report that they were duped? And why wouldn't Weizner let authorities know that his bottles of wine were being stolen?" the DA asked.

"If someone tells you that your million dollars' worth of wine is counterfeit, your choices are to take a hit, find out who, or forget about it. No one wants to take a loss, and over the last few months, Hans might have suspected that Andrew and the rest of the gang were stealing the counterfeit wine he made. Maybe he did murder Dave for the theft," Frisco said.

"How can you tell if a really old, ten thousand dollar bottle of Bordeaux for instance is real or fake?" Connor asked.

"No one in the world is able to authenticate via taste," I said. "This has been proven over and over again. Wine is a living thing, and it changes with time; no one knows what the original tasted like."

"So how were you able to tell?" the DA said.

"What you can do is what I did. I looked for inconsistencies in the bottle, the labels, and the corks to see if the wines were actually produced the year noted on the label, although it's harder to fake the newer, finer wines because many are outfitted with anti-counterfeit technology in the labels and bottles.

"One of the most highly counterfeited wines is 1945 Domain de la Romanee Conti. That wine was made into two barrels which made exactly six hundred bottles. These bottles have been found all over the world. A genuine bottle would be worth over a hundred thousand dollars."

"Why would anyone go to the trouble?"

"It's easy money. Ten to twenty thousand dollars a bottle, not easily caught, and it's an easy sell. There is a lot of one-upmanship, especially in buying rare wines."

"Well, at least there's not a lot of rare wine we have to worry about," Frisco added.

"Sorry, don't think it's just the high-rolling wine enthusiasts who are getting stung by counterfeiters. Some of your twenty-dollar bottles out there are also fake."

"Why is that?" the DA asked.

"You can produce them in vast quantities, and nobody is likely to catch you. If you figure fifty dollars a case and you move two hundred cases, then, yes, it's a pretty good living.

He smiled. "The theft of the 2000 Mission de Madonna Noire wine had possibilities if you had him nailed down."

"If you want to take down a big fish like Hans," he said looking directly at Frisco, "go get yourself a stick of dynamite or at least a bigger fishing rod."

I watched Frisco's jaw clench, and his veins were beginning to pop out of his neck. He said, "This isn't exactly my first rodeo."

Connor set his jaw. "And this isn't my first case, Frisco."

"I realize I'm not a detective, but I studied wine. I know the industry and the people in it. We're talking about three murders and the theft and forgery of wine," I interjected.

Frisco handed Connor the picture of the Weizner family. There was no mention of Hans being a part of the family. "If you remember, Daisy, at the estate there is a photograph of these same people on Hans Weizner's wall."

Connor studied the picture, then looked up at me. "You know what an adversarial expert witness would do with this? It's pure bullshit. You can't make a case with this flimsy stuff."

"He's in on it in some capacity, Connor," Frisco said firmly.

"Come back to me with something I can take to court and win with. Otherwise, have a nice day."

"How about a search and seizure of his wine?" Frisco suggested.

"Why?"

"Some crack whore can be arrested and held on suspicion of murder and theft. You bring in Weizner, you better arraign. If you let him know you believe he's a fraud and a murderer, you'll spend a lot of time fending off his lawyers. Unless, of course, he flees the country. Which he could. You need more evidence," Connor said.

"We have a partial print in the lab from Todd Burgess's murderer," Frisco said. "We also collected a coffee cup that Hans drank from."

"He's having another party; I'm sure to get an invitation if only out of curiosity at his competition. Of course, I don't think he knows that I'm the new owner because the house is still in Jack's name. Would you like to be my date for the occasion, Frisco?" Daisy asked.

He riveted his intense blue eyes at me. "I thought you'd never ask. I think we need to watch our backs, though."

"Are you sure it's him, Frisco?" Connor asked.

"He's linked to all three murders; he had motive, money, and means."

"Do you have trace evidence?" Connor asked.

"Yes, blood, but none of his was found at the crime scene. We have nothing in our database to prove it's Weizner's blood."

"There is nothing more I would like than for you to get the evidence on him," Conner said.

"When's the party, Daisy?"

"In two weeks. I'll have placed an ad in the paper about what's happening at the villa and ask if Jack will continue to let me use his name as the owner. It should make a good article and make Hans curious about the new one."

{ 42 }

*"For in the hand of the Lord there is a cup,
and the wine is red."*
PSALMS 75:8

I decided to make my vineyard organic; my reason was the health of not only the workers but of the land. Through my studies at Fresno State, I grew to believe that organically-grown grapes were superior to conventionally farmed grapes, and they made better wine. It was a win-win for everyone.

Hiking through the fields, I saw the men preparing the trellises. Although I was going to use Cabernet and Bordeaux to begin my vineyard, I had decided on Chardonnay as my grape of choice because of its role in producing the most excellent dry white wines in the world and the most exceptional sparkling wines, white Burgundies. It was also used as an everyday wine, which would make The Grey Stallion Winery viable in several markets.

Spotting José, I asked, "José, do you know if Charlotte ordered the French oak barrels?"

"Yes, Charlotte said they're expensive."

"The best Chardonnay means, at least for me, expensive barrels of French oak. Some of the other types of wine I plan on producing will be soaked in the oak chip, and for others, I will be adding the liquid essence of oak."

"Mr. Weizner does not use oak because he wants to replicate what the Italians, Austrians, and some of the French states are doing," said José.

"I am aware of what Mr. Weizner does, and I understand Charlotte's concern. As a competitor of his, we have to do something different, something more exotic. And wine drinkers like the flavor of Chardonnay. It's toasty, smoky, spicy, vanilla, or butterscotch. It's the oak barrel they perceive, not the grape."

"We are up near the mountains where it's a cooler temperature so the flavors will range. What do you want the flavor to be?" José asked.

"For our expensive wine, I'd like a dry, apple flavor. Our least expensive Chardonnay will be somewhat sweet, like tropical fruit. I want to go back to the old way of making wine, something that lives up to our name, although it's going to take a lot longer to ferment."

I heard a door creak open. "Wines that ferment in barrels actually end up tasting less oaky than wines that simply age in barrels, even though they might have spent more time in oak," Jack said. "Hi, hope I'm not interrupting anything here."

Surprised, I turned around. "No, José and I were just discussing the type of wine we're going to produce and how we're going to do it."

"Sounds like a heated debate."

"No, José has some strong, practical, tried and true opinions which are great, and I have many ideas that have not been put into a practical plan as yet. Makes for a good team," I said, smiling at José.

José returned my smile, waved goodbye to Jack, then headed to the field. "You've got a good man there and very smart," Jack said.

"I know, I'm lucky."

"Not so much lucky as smart. You saw Weizner's methods and are taking advantage of that knowledge."

"Thank you for all your help. I want to take this process slowly and make sure I'm doing everything right."

"How about if I help you?"

"You read my mind. I was going to ask if you would mind if I continued using your name as the owner of The Grey Stallion Winery. We can change the information later."

"Sure, that's not a problem. We can throw an advance party here to introduce a new locally-owned winery. You just need to tell me what you want to say in the article."

"Sure and if you get invited to Weizner's party in two weeks, will you let me go in your place?"

"Even better, I could go with you."

"Thanks, Jack, that sounds like a good idea. I've also invited Frisco."

"He's a good man, Daisy. By the way, have you put alarms in your home yet?"

"No, haven't had the time, but I plan to."

Smiling, he said, "First thing, I'm calling up my friend to have an alarm put in for the villa, for the tasting room, and I think on each of the farm worker's homes. Remember it has to look like I'm a big part of this place."

"Sounds great! Thank you, Jack."

"There have been three murders now, and you're assisting the detective in this. Weizner's going to be furious that his little intern and viticulturist is his number one competitor now that Dave is dead. It won't be safe when he finds out, if he is indeed the murderer," Jack said.

Jack was making a good argument. I didn't want any of my workers to be harmed because of me. "Okay, I would appreciate your assistance. For pay will you at least come for dinner once a week with me? We can discuss what we need to do in the future and about the wine."

Jack stuck out his hand for me to shake. "Sounds like a good deal if you can cook."

"No worries. You'll enjoy my food. It's take-out, but I do buy the best. Maybe you can barbecue now and again in the summer. I think it would also be an excellent time to sample our different wines."

"Do you know anything about the investigation and what or who the police suspect?" Jack asked.

I wasn't sure why he wanted to know about the investigation.

"I see that look on your face. I don't need to know. Just a small town, lots of gossip. I was curious. You don't need to say a thing to me," he added.

"Thank you."

"No problem, Daisy. When are you moving in?"

"I already have, but the furniture will be arriving tomorrow. It's going to be a long week."

"I'll leave and call the newspaper and my alarm company friend."

"See you later this week for dinner?"

"Count on it."

For some reason I suddenly felt uncomfortable. Someone once said that people who tried to ingratiate themselves into investigations only did so if they were guilty.

Could that be true of my own father?

{ 43 }

*"Making good wine is a skill;
making fine wine is an art."*
ROBERT MONDAVI

I was surprised when Frisco appeared at my home bearing gifts — a croissant and coffee. With profound glee and a look of wild-eyed elation and pride, he blurted out, "I think I know a way of outing Hans."

"Come on in. I'm drying my hair; it won't take but a minute. Freeway begged for some food, and it looked like Frisco might give in.

Too excited to sit, Frisco paced in my bedroom while I finished with my hair. He unfolded a microfiche copy of an old German newspaper with an article and Hans's picture in it. I didn't read German or speak it, but Frisco had it translated for the both of us. I watched him circle around the room, trying to keep up the pace while reading the article to me.

"AP 2000. Kurt Klemper, thief, con-man, and exposed imposter who was convicted of stalking the Weizner family members and was known to have stolen a bottle of the famous Mission de Madonna Noire wine, escaped prison yesterday. He is a dangerous criminal so be on the lookout. Do not try and apprehend him."

"Oh, my God, that is Hans! I knew he was a thief. Can we take this information to the District Attorney? Do you think he will give us a search warrant to go into the lab? Then we can make the beaker that we took legal."

"I think this will help the DA convict Hans of forgery, but we still don't have any evidence to tie him to the murders. We do, however, have enough to begin having him watched."

Finishing up my hair and makeup, I walked over to the couch and picked up the cup of coffee and croissant. "Do you want something to eat?"

"I need something to drink. Do you have any juice?"

I pointed to the refrigerator. "Help yourself."

After he decided on orange juice and potato chips, he sat next to me and spread out his notebook. I scooped up Freeway, and she settled down between us.

"Why did you decide to look at the German paper? That had to have taken a lot of research," I asked.

"It was something Savannah said recently about Hans seeming a little questionable to her. She wondered why he didn't speak more about his family and his country. That got me to thinking. If he committed crimes here, surely he had done something before. I began searching the Internet, and I found out about the theft of a fifty thousand dollar bottle of wine from Switzerland. I dug deeper and saw a picture of Hans but with the name Wilhelm Klinsman. Everything began to fall into place after that."

"He uses several aliases, and if he counterfeits the 2000 Mission de Madonna Noire, it pencils out to eight thousand dollars per glass," I said in amazement.

"We don't have him yet." Frisco shook his head, taking a swallow of his juice. "All of the information — the wine, the newspaper article, the picture — is only circumstantial."

"So what do we need to do next?"

"We need to tie Hans to one or all of the murders and take the contents of the barrel of wine from the cellar and compare them to Dave Brinker's wine in case there was a reason that Brinker was killed because of the wine."

"I have a diary that I've kept information in. I'll go get it." I went to the bedroom and reached into my bag and pulled out the brown-covered book.

I handed the notebook to Frisco. I began looking through all of his documentation.

We spent the rest of the day hunched over reports. I wanted Hans to be caught but perversely maybe not. He did commit the theft, but did he have something to do with the murders? I'd also like to know if he was the one who broke into my room.

Frisco looked up from my notebook. "This is it. This is how we're going to bring him in."

{ 44 }

"For when the wine is in, the wit is out."
TOMAS BACON

"So what's the plan?" I asked him.

"You have in your diary that Hans Weizner had a lunch meeting with Dave Brinker the day Dave died. There are also records I retrieved from Todd Burgess's cell showing numerous calls to and from Hans."

"If no murder had occurred, it would seem like everyday business. Except he should have had no business with Todd because Todd was Dave's employee. Todd was also Andrew's friend. At least, I think they were."

"No, Daisy, they weren't friends; they were co-conspirators. We found this uncashed check in Todd's room for a hundred thousand dollars signed by Brinker. And we know Todd had a meeting with Andrew. Remember I saw Brinker pass an envelope to Todd. Maybe it was a payoff," Frisco said.

Mr. Weizner lived a life under many guises. Like Hans, I kept my own dark secrets, protecting myself from a life I never wanted to return to. I was happy with the new me. I still didn't know what happened to my mom. I never heard from her except that one note that she may have sent. I was hiding from my past.

Frisco seemed like an easy going man. His daughter was his life. He just did what he was supposed to do. I wonder if he knew about my mother, would he still want to date me? He lived a good life and had a successful career. Something was missing, though. He stepped closer and ran his thumb along my cheek.

"Perhaps you are the one to keep me going. Will you lead me down a new path? Or will you leave me one day, Daisy?"

"I would never hurt you, Frisco, or your daughter." I meant this with all my heart. He was the one, my true love, but he was so much dearer to me than that. His every touch that sent my body tingling was only a small fraction of what I felt for him.

{ 45 }

"A man not old, but mellow, like good wine."
STEPHEN PHILLIPS

I promised Jack I would stop by his friend's antique store, aptly called "A Step Back in Time" and owned by Milly Preston, an elderly woman with sharp black eyes that seemed to drill a hole through me, giving me a comfort level of a negative number.

"You do a lot of looking and not much buying," said Milly. "I'm not sure if you noticed that this is a place of commerce and not a museum."

"Ah, well, I want to be sure of what I buy and if it fits my style," I said, picking up an antique tea set.

"Really? I don't have matching cheetah print pillows for your couch if that's what you're looking for."

"So what you're saying is that my style seems to be animal print?" This is a friend of Jack's? I think she might be an acquired taste.

"I don't get many young visitors at this store, let alone ones who buy so many random things. Unless you're buying my stuff to open your own antique store. If that's the case, then just buy the store, and I'll be done with it."

"Is the store for sale?"

"What?"

"Your store. Is it for sale?"

"No."

"I think we're getting off on the wrong foot. I'm buying stuff for my home. It's just across from Jack Fletcher's place," I said.

"Yes, I know the place. It was owned by Jack's family. After his wife left him, taking their little girl, he didn't want the place after that. It's been sitting empty ever since."

"It looks well cared for."

"That's Jack and the caretaker he hired." I think she thought that explained everything.

"Do you know why she left?" I asked.

"Who?"

"Jack's wife?" I was beginning to feel that the conversation with this lady was like chasing my own tail.

"The way I hear it, she was crazy, didn't like working on a farm with horses and building up a winery."

"That's very sad. I've invited Jack over for dinner once a week in exchange for his offer to help me."

"I'd say you're getting the better end of the offer. He knows a lot about the land, the vendors, the types of grapes grown around here, and he's a good friend to have."

"Umm, you've got a point. Is this tea set for sale?"

"Which one is that?"

"It has blue and purple flowers and looks very old."

"That was Jack's grandmother's tea set. It was an arranged marriage or so I'm told. Cruz Mendez was his name. He lived in Milpitas. Worked hard all his life, finally marrying Viola. The flowers on the cups are violets. Cruz bought the set as a wedding gift to her. Now that I've given you some history, I'm glad you're buying something instead of loitering."

"Does crankiness come with age?"

"Like the finest wines, dearie."

I drove home, pleased with all my new stuff, a feeling that lasted until I saw who was in my driveway.

{ 46 }

"Here's the corkscrew —
a useful key to unlock the storehouse of wit,
the treasury of laughter, the front door of fellowship, and the
gate of pleasant folly."
W.E.P. FRENCH

Hey, you hungry?" Frisco lifted a bag of burgers up high so I could see it.

"I'm starved. What are you doing here?" The sky was still light. I was able to see Frisco's face quite clearly and was surprised by the handsomeness of his features. Dark hair, firm jaw, excellent bone structure, and beautiful eyes.

"It's about the murders."

I tensed up. I was afraid, and I didn't mind admitting it.

"Let's go inside, Frisco. The hamburgers smell delicious. Are there fries? What do you want to discuss about the case?"

"Here's a soda, and yes, some fries. Where do I set it?" Frisco asked.

"Kitchen counter will work until I get additional chairs for the table."

"We found the knife that was used to kill Todd Burgess," Frisco said between a handful of fries.

"Where did you find it?"

"A dad with his son were fishing near town, and the boy hooked a large bass. When the dad went to scoop it up, he got a surprise as well, a KA-Bar-TDI knife."

"That's pretty lucky."

"And he knew there had been a murder so he called our department. Sanchez went out to pick it up."

"How can you be sure the knife is the one that killed Todd?"

"It fits the ME's description."

"Was it also the weapon that killed Andrew?"

"It's highly likely, but we won't know for sure until the ME checks it out."

"Do you think there's another murderer and maybe in the sheriff's department?"

"Possibly. We checked out Dave Brinker because he was in the police force years ago. I might have to give him a second look."

"Maybe there is more than one killer."

"Could be. Hans could still have murdered Dave."

"I didn't think about that." Probably because my desire for Frisco addled my brain.

We finished eating our burger and fries. The hair on Frisco's arm gently grazed against mine. My stomach flip-flopped.

I looked at him. I wanted to take him upstairs and was pretty sure he wanted to go. Unfortunately, just as we leaned toward each other, the phone rang.

"It's Sanchez. I got to go. It looks like something else has materialized."

Dammit. Sometimes cell phones can really dampen the mood.

{ 47 }

"If God forbade drinking, would he have made it so good?"
CARDINAL RICHELEU

The furniture arrived the next day, as did the cranky lady with the tea set.

"Jesus, this place is gloomy. Why don't you put some headstones next to the front door? That'll really bring in the yuppies."

"That's a great idea. Can I borrow yours? But you didn't need to come all the way out here to deliver the tea set," I said.

Milly looked wistfully over her shoulder at Jack's place.

"Aww, I get it," I said. "Would you like me to brew up some tea? I could invite Jack over for a cup and to see the tea set."

"Do you think I have nothing to do all day but drink tea? No, thank you, Daisy."

"So you have something else better to do like yelling at the one customer you will have today?"

Milly pursed her lips and glared at me. "Mmm, I'll take the silence as a no." I called Jack.

He answered on the first ring. "I saw Milly's car. Do you need any help?"

"No help needed but would like to have you over for a cup of tea."

"Thank you. I'll get my boots on and be right over."

While we waited, I let Milly wander around the house. I told her some ideas I had on how to furnish my mostly empty downstairs.

"I think a mahogany coffee table with Tiffany in-laid glass would look good near the fireplace. Maybe oriental chairs, bookcases, and an overstuffed sofa."

"Hey, I think I've seen this room before. It's on page twenty-two of the Pottery Barn catalog," Milly yelled out from across the room.

"Hi, Jack. What do you have there?"

"I purchased some lamps from Milly for a housewarming gift. I saw them in the back seat of her car and thought I'd bring them in for her," Jack said.

"I knew I recognized your voice." Milly came down the stairs, wagging a finger Jack's way. "How've you been, Jack?"

"Not too bad, Milly. How are you?"

"I'm okay," Milly sighed, looking at Jack.

"Milly and I went to Yosemite High together many years ago."

"Seems like yesterday, Jack."

I shouldn't be here. I was intruding on a special moment. I wondered if it would be awkward to tell them to get a room.

I heard the teapot whistle. "Tea's ready. What would you like in yours?"

"Here, let me," Milly said, picking up the teapot.

"Who are you and what have you done with the Milly I met?" I asked under my breath.

Jack picked up the teacup and examined it. A smile broke across his face. "Did you buy this, Daisy?"

"Yep. It's beautiful, and it spoke to me."

"This is my family's set."

"Milly told me. I'm glad to have this little bit of history of our family."

Smiling, he looked across at me. "I'm glad, too."

"Are you two related?" Milly asked.

"Yes, Milly, this is my daughter."

"Sure took you long enough to get back up here," she exclaimed.

And the witch is back, I thought.

José came into the kitchen and asked me to come out to the vineyard because they needed a decision made regarding the barrels.

I excused myself. Milly picked up her purse to leave.

"No, you guys stay here awhile. I'll be right back. I enjoy your company," I said.

"Do you need any help with the barrels?" Jack asked.

"At this moment, no. Finish your tea, and I'll be back before you're done." Unless of course, they were no longer in my living room, in which case I certainly wasn't going to go look for them.

{ 48 }

"Drink no longer water, but use a little wine for the stomach's sake and thine often information."
1 TIMOTHY 5:23

Why do you need help with the barrels?" I asked, because José rarely needed my help with anything so I was a little confused.

"I don't. I thought I should get this information to you only. The vines you chose were delivered, but I'm afraid you received the cuttings that mature more slowly, and they aren't a fruit-flavored blend."

"How's that possible? I went in there personally and picked out the clonal selection."

"Why's that? I could have done it," José stated.

"With this particular variety their fruit grows slightly faster and produces grapes with a slightly different aroma and flavor than this other one that was delivered. I have to start planting now. This could be a disaster for me."

"How can I help?"

"Call the store back. I want to return these and get the ones I ordered."

"I tried, but they said that you'd called them and changed the order so they went to Weingart."

I wheeled around, leaving José and walked into my home, slamming the door behind me.

Milly and Jack looked up in surprise. "You offered me help, Jack. I know it was for moving the furniture, but the order of vines I purchased was not delivered. They told José that my grapes were going to Hans Weizner. Can you do anything about this?"

Jack pulled out his cell. "Hi, Pete, Jack here. I just found out that my neighbor's grapes were taken by someone. How soon can you get the grapes she ordered out here? Yes, I understand, but she did not change the order. Have you sent them to Weingart Winery yet? Good. Please get Daisy's grapes out here no later than tomorrow morning. She has a crew ready to plant. Next time this happens make sure you call her for verification. Yes, Pete, this was a dirty trick that you got pulled into. I'm sure it won't happen again."

"Jack, you got them?"

"Your order will be out before lunchtime, so you won't be paying the men for nothing."

I was so relieved. "Thank you, Jack. Did Pete verify that it was Hans who tried to scoop up my grapes?"

"Competition can be a nasty thing."

"If it weren't for all the competition in town, I'd be a millionaire," Milly said.

I had to bite my tongue on that one. If Milly were more helpful, she'd make a few more bucks. Instead, I said, "That was a shitty thing to do. Hans is worried. Good! It seems like he is capable of just about anything."

"That's what has me concerned. I ordered the alarms for your home, but I haven't installed them yet. Did you call anyone?"

"No, I was going to do it this weekend."

"I need to get back to my store," Milly said.

Jack walked over to Milly and helped her up. They walked arm-in-arm to her car, talking and laughing. It was good to see. Maybe they would go out together. Perhaps I could help that along with a dinner party I planned to throw and invite the community under Jack's name. I wasn't able to compete head to head with Weingart Winery, but maybe we could get the community behind us in Oakhurst.

{ 49 }

"There is a devil in every berry of the grape."
THE KORAN

Frisco called me into the precinct. We were going to keep a close eye on Weizner. Frisco had yet to find out who the killer was or the plant that poisoned Dave Brinker.

I knew Mr. Weizner liked to brag about the wine to prove to people that he'd outsmarted the best connoisseurs of wine. I decided to drive back to my home since I wasn't going to be a part of the surveillance team.

Entering the wine tasting room with its attractive brick wall, I saw Charlotte speaking with Mrs. Wright, the mayor of Oakhurst whom I had once served in Mr. Weizner's tasting room.

"Good afternoon, Mayor Wright. What a pleasant surprise," I said.

"Oh, Daisy, I'm so happy for you. I knew from the first day we met that one day you would be a success. I'm so glad it's up here in Oakhurst with us. I just wanted you to know that I'm good friends with the chefs at the Tenaya Lodge and Yosemite Hotel," she said, bursting with energy. "I thought it might be a wonderful idea if we held a tasting of your wine when it becomes available."

I looked over at Charlotte. She was smiling. "I can't thank you enough, Mayor; this is wonderful. I want you to know how happy I am to be here with so many kind people."

"You are so welcome," the Mayor said with a grin.

"Well, I have to be on my way. I have so many stops and so many people to see. I also have a quilter's meeting tonight. You should come with me one night."

"I have never been able to sew, quilt, or do anything with a needle. I'm a failure I'm afraid, but I would love to bring wine to one of your events."

"Then it becomes a party, and I think many of the women will appreciate the wine. If not, let them drink tea," she said with a giggle.

After she left, Charlotte and I went into her office. "What is it, Daisy?"

"I just had a few more questions for you."

"Regarding what? Oh, you mean Hans," Charlotte asked, looking down at her hands.

"Yes. You kept the books, right?"

"You know I did," she answered stiffly.

"Let's just talk for a minute, put our heads together. You worked for Hans for some years. Do you believe he is capable of murder? Was there anything in his books, maybe a payout that you didn't know anything about?"

She shrugged her shoulders, exasperated. "Yes, there were large checks, but I assumed they were for something for the vineyard."

"Sounds plausible but now under the circumstances do you think any of them could be for blackmail?"

"A check would have to be written to someone and I'd see that when reconciling the checkbook against the bank so I doubt it. Wait, I do remember Hans being furious on one occasion. He slammed through my office door and told me to drop everything and write him a check for one hundred thousand dollars. Even though I tried to question him, he just told me to get back to my work."

"Can you remember the date or close to the date that you gave him the check?"

"At the beginning of the year. After you came on board."

"How do you remember that?"

"Mr. Weizner made a nasty comment about my choice of work attire." She looked away. When she turned back, her eyes filled up with tears.

"I asked him why he was so angry. He's completely messed up, Daisy. Maybe he had a bad childhood. He's trying to make his business work. He cuts corners. And there's something else, Daisy, but I don't want to get into it."

"What could you have done, Charlotte?"

"I kept a second set of books in case Hans threatened me. I was afraid of the man."

"You need to give those records to Frisco immediately. Why didn't you give them earlier with the investigation going on?"

"What I did wasn't ethical. I didn't want the police to suspect me of anything."

"I'll call Frisco and let him know you're on your way to his office. You can have the rest of the day off, Charlotte." I wasn't happy with this bit of information and wondered what else she was holding back.

{ 50 }

"Wine gives us liberty, love takes it away.
Wine makes us princes, love makes us beggars."
WYCHERLY

Frisco, the D.A., the captain, and Sanchez were present at the police station within three hours' notice.

"Madera County is ready to indict Weizner," Frisco told me. Charlotte had given Frisco the second set of records, and he had presented them to DA Connor.

"I can't believe Charlotte had a second copy of the accounting books when Weizner told us to go fish," I said.

"It's another missing piece of the puzzle that we needed to tie him to the theft of the wine and the murder of Dave Brinker. I think this will tie the killings together and is the reason behind the murders," Frisco said.

"What I'm afraid of is that he will leave the country with his German passport," Sanchez commented.

"I think we need to move quickly to bring him in with the evidence we have on him," the DA said.

"What do the books show?" questioned Ochoa.

"They show payouts to a chemist for one."

"This seems a little too convenient. What proof do you have to back up the books? For all we know Charlotte doctored them," said Ochoa.

"That's a possibility, but do you have enough evidence to bring Weizner in? We don't want to scare him off. Another thing to think about is if he murdered Todd. I don't think you have enough evidence for that."

"I don't want to lose the only suspect still alive," Frisco said.

I sat and watched the wheels turn in the investigation and looked at the perp board. All of a sudden it hit me. The last person to see Dave alive was

Hans. They'd had a meal together at Timothy's Restaurant. "Did you find a castor plant or anything that could be made into poison?" I asked.

"Who served the food?" Sanchez asked.

"According to Timothy's statement, he did. He said there were no mushrooms served that night with their dishes so we need to look for someone who had knowledge of the castor plant," Frisco said.

"We need a search warrant for Hans's home, and we need to find out more about Dave's knife. Where and when he got it. If it had something to do with blackmail," Sanchez said.

Frisco said, "I'll get a search warrant for Dave's home and for the banks. Sanchez, when you checked out Todd and Andrew's banks, did you see if there were large deposits, maybe a security vault that they left the money in, or maybe just one did?"

"I did check, and there was only one large deposit, and it was placed in Charlotte's account."

"Was it a joint account? If so, is the money still there?" I asked.

"I don't think so, but I'm not sure."

"Get a search warrant for Charlotte's accounts," Frisco said to Sanchez.

Later that afternoon Dave's lawyer showed up at the Brinker home. Frisco handed the lawyer the warrant to search the premises again.

The sheriff began to pace while waiting for the lawyer to read through each page very slowly.

"You need to remain in the rooms that this court order states. Everything else is off limits."

"This is an investigation into Dave's death. I would think you would want to know what happened," Frisco said.

The lawyer shook his head in exacerbation. "That isn't my call."

Where would Dave have hidden information on the knife? If they couldn't find anything, Frisco would check with the sheriff's department to take a look at their records regarding weapons assigned to each deputy. "I'm going to his office to look over his receipts for purchases in the last year five years," Frisco said.

Frisco headed into the bedroom, then sat at Dave's desk. He rummaged through the drawers and checked under the desk. The desk was an antique; he'd seen others like this that had hidden compartments so he checked for those. He tried every drawer, every opening, until he stumbled upon a drawer that when pulled open, had a lever inside.

The lawyer gripped the edge of the desk. "What the hell are you doing? What's in there?"

{ 51 }

"It is well that there are five reasons for drinking: the arrival of a friend; one's present or future thirst, the excellence of the wine; or any other reason."
LATIN SAYING

"I think I found a hidden compartment! How about you open it so I don't have to break the drawer?" Frisco asked the lawyer.

The lawyer walked over with a set of keys and finally found the right one to unlock the hidden drawer. Inside was a receipt for a knife with a new KA-Bar-TDI resting on top.

Frisco pounded the desk. "Well, that answers part of the puzzle. If his old knife was gone, he'd want another."

"What did you find?" Captain Ochoa asked.

"You're not going to believe it. Come here and take a look."

Ochoa dropped what he was doing and ran over to see what Frisco had. "This bible is hollowed out, and there's a diary inside."

"What does it say?" Ochoa took it from Frisco and opened it.

"It begins when he took over the estate after his parents died." Ochoa turned page after page, and Frisco listened to what had happened in Dave's life and his struggles. All he had left was the land so he took out a second mortgage to pay his wife's medical bills, but the bank was about to foreclose on him. I almost feel sorry for him," Ochoa said. "He was a good cop. Later I heard his wife died."

"He met Andrew through Todd. They went out drinking, shot pool. One evening Andrew's wife had Dave, Todd, and Charlotte over for dinner. Andrew got royally drunk and told the group about wine that Weizner stole in France. Andrew complained that he was getting screwed out of money, but he was the one who had done all of the work. He wanted a more significant cut, or he was going to steal the bottles away from Hans and sell them under a different label."

"So what happened? What changed?"

"I don't think anything necessarily changed. What happened was Andrew stole the wine from Weizner and gave it to Dave Brinker. Dave and Todd changed the labels on them and sold Dave's new wine for less than Weizner. They made a killing."

"Not smart. Dave was an ex-cop; he knew better than to write all this stuff down."

"Look at the date. It is after Andrew's death. Maybe he was being threatened and wrote it down just in case," said Frisco.

"Do you think Dave killed anyone?" Ochoa asked.

"I don't think so; he was trying to save his home and land."

"I think this is where he really begins to unravel. Dave inherited the land and didn't know much about wines, vines, or grapes, and Weizner knew that."

"Weizner was at the party so he didn't have the opportunity to go downstairs and kill Andrew. Someone else is the murderer. Maybe Weizner had a partner."

"So now there's a mystery person. Who murdered Andrew and Todd?"

"Dave trusted no one and thought that Todd might go to the police. Dave confronted Todd outside the Medical Examiner's office where I saw him pass off an envelope."

"What was in it?" Captain Ochoa asked.

"According to Todd's bank statement, it was money for Todd, enough to leave town, get a new start, and never come back. And Todd did take the money."

"So if Dave paid Todd off and Todd left town, Dave wouldn't have any reason to kill him."

"You're right. Dave isn't the killer. Todd had no reason to kill anyone, nor did Andrew."

"So it's back to Weizner or the mystery person."

{ 52 }

"Drink wine, and you will sleep well. Sleep, and you will not sin. Avoid sin, and you will be saved. Ergo, drink wine and be saved."
MEDIEVAL GERMAN SAYING

It was close to daybreak when a cool breeze drifted through my window and chilled me. I bundled up in a blanket and folded myself into my chair.

Off in the distance I could see the lights of Fresno as people got up from their beds to go to work.

There was a knock at the front door. "Daisy, you in there?"

"Yes, hang on." I could smell the coffee, or was I dreaming it?"

"Thank you! I could get used to this." I smiled. It felt right, like before I had been missing a piece of me, and now I felt whole.

Frisco sat next to me gazing at the sunrise. "I don't want this moment to end, Daisy."

I could sense the heat in his gaze signified more than admiration.

I couldn't help but smile. He brushed up against me. I felt chills go up my arms. I didn't want it to end either.

{ 53 }

"Either give me more wine or leave me alone."
JALALUDDIN MEVLANA RUMI

After Frisco left for the precinct, I went to my home office and picked up Charlotte's accounting ledger for the purchases we made for The Grey Stallion Winery. Sitting down in the chair, I began perusing the numbers. Something struck me. I couldn't quite put my finger on it, but I knew something was wrong.

My coat pocket began to vibrate. "Hi, Daisy speaking."

"Hi, Daisy. We're a few weeks away from The Grey Stallion's grand opening. Can you come over to taste some food we're preparing for the party? I'd also like to show you the stemware and have you help us marry the wine with the right food."

"Sure, I'll be over this afternoon."

"About two o'clock would be perfect."

I marked the appointment in my phone and walked over to the bin that held wine made at Fresno State. I wanted to sell this in my tasting room to support the college.

I picked up my purse and got a call. It was Frisco. That put a smile on my face.

"I need you down here." The smile left my face.

"What is going on?"

"It's about the case."

I drove down Highway 41 to Madera County Sheriff's office. When I arrived, Frisco was standing outside waiting for me.

"Sanchez found vials in Hans's safe and the ledger. I thought you'd like to go to the lab with me."

"Yes, thank you for including me," I said appreciatively, but his next statement threw me.

"Where did you say you were from?" He watched me in fascination, unable to take his eyes off my face. He's roused the passion that lay dormant within me for years. It was so hard to trust, and yet I believed Frisco with all my heart.

"My birth certificate says that I'm from Oakhurst. Why?"

"Where did you grow up then?" he asked.

"I don't think I ever said, but I was raised in Inglewood, California."

"Were you involved in a murder?"

"My mother killed my stepfather, Mike Murphy. She took off before the police caught her. I was put in juvenile hall for helping her and then foster care until I was eighteen." We kept walking to the lab.

"Things seem to be a little too coincidental. Murder seems to follow you. I don't believe in coincidences."

"And they said you couldn't teach old dogs new tricks." It was like someone threw a bucket of cold water on me.

I turned to leave. "You have no idea what you're talking about. I can't believe you'd think I was a murderer or that I had anything to do with these murders." I wiped my eyes and tried to say more, but the words were choked up deep down inside of me.

I swung around and left for home. He didn't even give me a chance to explain "It's not what you think, Frisco." I wanted nothing more to do with the case. It was leading me down a rabbit hole that I had been trying to dig myself out of for a long time. I flung open the truck door and raced home. I ran up the stairs, and it was like a dam busted. I couldn't hold back the tears. I cuddled Freeway, rocking her until I fell asleep. I really didn't know what happened between Frisco and me. I was going to tell him about my past.

Hours later the house was dark. I felt like I had been run over by a freight train. I walked into the kitchen, then jumped back. "What are you doing here, Jack?"

"I was worried and thought I'd stay down here until you were ready to talk and see if I could help you."

"That's a little above and beyond the call of duty, but I'll take a cup of that coffee you're brewing."

"You and I used to talk over coffee when you were little."

"What?" I was sure I didn't hear him right. "Mom wouldn't have let you give me coffee."

"I used to fill the cup with a little bit of coffee, lots of milk and sugar, and we used to sit outside together on the porch."

"In the back of my mind, I had a feeling that you were my dad from the first day we met. The daisy bushes on your property were clues, too. And I do remember the coffee and lots of sugar and cream."

"I never wanted to interfere with you and your mom all these years. I stayed in the background, but I went to all of your special events. I was at your graduation from both high school and college. I watched you at many of the football games when you were cheering."

"I think I need to sit down." I grabbed onto a table and maneuvered myself into a chair.

"I'd like to believe you needed me, but no, if you're honest with yourself, you never really needed me until now. You need to know about Mike."

"I already know, Jack."

"I don't believe you really do."

The lights were on inside the house. He was parked in the driveway. He sat waiting and watching. There would one day be an opportunity. Daisy had it too good.

{ 54 }

"Wine ... cheerth God and man."
JUDGES 9:13

I know it's been difficult, Daisy. I know that you did not kill Mike, but like it or not you were involved."

"I called the cops. I buried Mike. What else could I do? Mom completely lost it, and I didn't want her to go to prison. She needed help."

"You did everything you could. You couldn't have stopped your mom; you were a kid. She should have been taking care of you, not the other way around. And because of you the police found Mike before he died. He had partially gotten himself out of the hole you had dug. Mike's gunshot wound went through to his skill. He was taken to the hospital, and before the cops could question him, he ran away."

"Oh, my God! I've lived with this guilt for so long. Why didn't you come and take me away from her? You knew where we were. I'd have been a lot better off with you than with her or in a foster home."

"I tried to get her help, but she insisted that I was crazy and needed help, not her. Mike is not dead. Your mom is still wanted for attempted murder."

"Wait a minute; he's not dead! You're positive?"

"He survived, and according to the papers, he did not remember what happened to him."

"Is he back with Mom?"

"No, but he's out there. That's why I continued to watch out for you from a distance and insisted on the alarm. Has your mom contacted you since you've lived here? Did she visit you at college?"

"No, but she did write me once, at least I think she did."

"Daisy, there is no easy way to say this. I'm sorry, but your mom was murdered a few days ago. I just saw it in the paper. They don't know who did it yet, but he had to be familiar to her since she let him into her home."

"Oh, my God, I loved her. Why didn't she ever visit me?"

"I have no idea why, honey."

"Who could have murdered her?"

"Daisy, I don't know the answer to that, but in her own way your mom loved you."

"I should have tried to find her. Call her, something."

"At one time she was a wonderful, caring wife and mother to you, but she became sick."

I didn't want to believe what I was hearing. I tried to put my hands over my ears and pretend all of this was a nightmare. "How did he survive?"

"I have no idea, Daisy. You may want to speak to the police. I'm sure they have heard something about it."

"I think I need time to process all of this. Why didn't you ever come and get me, take me away, and bring me back here with you? Maybe this is why Frisco was asking me all of his questions."

"She wouldn't let me have you, and back then men didn't have the rights that they do now in getting custody of their children. I was ordered to stay away by the courts. She accused me of so many things. The courts believed her. I was there for every event, every graduation, and the scholarship to Fresno State, but I had to keep my distance."

"You could have tried to get me before I was placed in foster care, couldn't you?"

{ 55 }

"A man cannot make him laugh — but that's no marvel; he drinks no wine."
SHAKESPEARE

I was both mentally and physically tired. Mike was not dead. I was relieved but anxious. I knew my part in the crime only too well. My mom dragged me into that mess. She was guilty of a crime. It was not self-defense according to my dad. And when I really needed my dad, he stayed at a distance. This was a lot to take in and process.

I picked up Freeway and took her out for a walk into the fields. It was an incredible site. The land in the San Joaquin Valley is the most fertile in the United States. It grows a full sixty per cent of all the agricultural products in California. I'm happy, content with my life here. Maybe that's all there will ever be for me.

I saw José and waved at him. We decided a few days ago to add ten acres of generic blended grape because we needed a cheap wine to sell for our basic bread and butter.

The night was slowly turning colder. I was getting hungry, and I thought about calling Frisco but decided that he had every right to want to keep his distance from me.

Freeway and I walked back home. I grabbed a bottle of Chablis and a hunk of cheese. Walking out to the patio that overlooked the valley, I sat and gazed out. My mom was murdered by someone, and the Mike I thought was dead was actually alive. I wondered if he was looking for me.

{ 56 }

"Wine is bottled poetry."
ROBERT LOUIS STEVENSON

"I have news," Frisco said.

I thought I should hang up, but I didn't. Some part of me was still hopeful.

"I thought you might be interested to know that Sanchez found a connection to the murder of Dave. Would you be interested in coming down to the precinct? Katie was your friend who disappeared, right? You've been a part of this investigation from the beginning; you might want to be here for the end."

"Actually, you thought wrong. I'm overwhelmed and just sad right now. I'll read about it in the papers."

I hung up the phone and left for the tasting room to see Charlotte.

"Good morning, Charlotte," I said.

Looking up from the computer screen, Charlotte slid her glasses off her face and smiled. "How are you this morning?"

"Fine." If I didn't count my throbbing head. "I thought I'd go over my new ideas for the party. What do you think?"

"I think it's a great idea. So many of the companies forget the locals and just look to invite the dignitaries, which is silly. There are a lot more regular people than there are mayors, board members, and the like. The word would spread much faster. How can I help you with this?"

"I hope to meet with the catering company on Thursday. Would you like to come?"

"Yes, thank you."

Now that that was done, Freeway and I left for the fields, but halfway to the fields I spotted Frisco's truck pulling into my driveway.

"I need to talk to you, Daisy!"

I turned in a different direction. I didn't want to talk to him. At least not yet.

He apparently had other ideas as he ran up and grabbed my arm. "You're not going anywhere."

{ 57 }

"Poetry is devils' wine."
ST. AUGUSTINE

"Let go of my arm." He didn't, so I slugged him.

"Listen to me, please, Daisy," Frisco said.

"I really don't know what more you could add to the discussion we last had."

"I'm sorry, Daisy."

"No, it's my fault. I wanted to tell you everything but was afraid. I should have trusted you."

"I know. I had a talk with Jack last night. I did believe that you were mixed up in this in some way. Jack set me straight and even offered to kick my butt."

"He did?"

"Yes, but I'm wondering why a neighbor would care that much about you."

"It's not that complicated, Frisco. I found out about three months ago that

Jack is my dad. I was born here, but my mother took me away. I haven't seen him since I was six years old."

"So why wasn't he there for you?" Frisco asked.

"He told me that there was a court order mandating he stay away from me, though he said he came to important events in my life."

"Did you see him?"

"No, but before you ask, I don't think I would've recognized him. I'd like to trust that he did. I'd like to have faith that he cares about me and wants me to succeed. Otherwise, why would he bother to try to straighten things out?"

"I get your point. Honestly, Daisy, I was afraid of caring too much for you and that maybe you'd leave me."

"I fight for those I love and believe in."

"Wait, did you just say you loved me? I love you too, Daisy. We both need to work on our trust issues. But I want us to work. I want us to have a relationship." Frisco put both his arms around me, and it felt so good.

"I'd like that as well. You came here for another reason, or is Jack's threat the reason?"

"I wanted you to know that Hans is in a holding cell at the precinct. He has a lawyer, and in the next hour he will be arraigned. Would you like to be there with me?"

"We've been partners throughout so yes, I'd like to be there with you, Frisco."

I got into his truck, and we drove to the courthouse. Sitting there and looking at Hans, he didn't have the look of a guilty man. He seemed confident that he would be back at his estate in time to pull his wine tasting event together.

"I may be guilty of some things, Your Honor, but murder is not one of them." He smiled — the same confident smile that I remembered from when I'd first met him.

"Where were you when Dave was murdered?" the District Attorney asked.

"I'm not sure. What time was that supposed to have happened?"

"Let me refresh your memory. It was just after the two of you had lunch together."

"Ah, yes, I went home and didn't see him after that day."

What were you and Dave discussing? We have witnesses who claim you were in a heated discussion at the restaurant."

"I accused him of being a thief."

"Did you steal the original wine from France that you now call Madonna Maria?"

"No, I did not. Andrew did."

"Yet you are the one with all the cases of wine in your lab. It looks like there is a million dollars' worth of wine there. Was Dave rebottling it? Putting his own label on the bottles and selling them to unwary people?"

"Yes; at our dinner he freely admitted that he, Andrew, and Todd stole my wine. That does not make me a murderer."

"True, but how do you explain the vials of ricin that we found in your bank safe?"

"I can't explain it. Maybe you should talk to Charlotte!"

"Your Honor, since Mr. Weizner came of his own free will to the precinct, I think we can show him some courtesy," Hans's Defense Attorney said. "As you can well imagine he's in a bit of shock after losing his friend Dave and then the suddenness of such an accusation that he was the murderer doesn't help. It's not even plausible, particularly since Mr. Weizner has been complying with the investigation and answering questions."

"Thank you, Mr. Rogers. I will render a decision within the hour."

"Thank you, Your Honor."

"I didn't kill Dave. This is crazy. Someone else did it." Hans looked at me. "You could have killed all of these people, Daisy. You're trying to stick it to me. I didn't do it. My reputation is down the toilet, and you caused it."

Something else was going on. Frisco took hold of my hand. It wasn't reassuring because as I looked at Hans I began to panic. Who had access to Hans's accounting books, his money, his friends, his ... Was it Charlotte?

I tried to stand up to leave, but my head began to swirl, and I was on the verge of a panic attack. I needed a paper bag to breathe in.

"Daisy, are you okay?" Frisco asked.

I was panting. I got up and ran out the door. I made it to the bathroom before dry heaving.

Frisco pounded on the door, shouting for me. I just needed a moment to settle myself down. I willed myself to breathe in slowly, and gradually I began to calm down. Someone else killed those three men, someone they knew and trusted. Did Charlotte do it for Hans?

{ 58 }

"...the odour of Burgundy, and the smell of French sauces, and the sight of clean napkins and long loves, knocked as a very welcome visitor at the door of our inner man."
JEROME K. JEROME

Hans was taken back to his cell to await the judge's decision.

I came out of the bathroom and paced, looking for Frisco. My head felt like it was about to explode.

"What's wrong, Daisy?" he asked. "We got him, and he's in a cell where he can't hurt anyone anymore."

"Something is wrong, Frisco. We need to go back over the evidence. Can we go to the precinct and look back over the timeline and where everyone was? I've got a gnawing feeling in my gut."

"We can go, but what's your thinking?"

At the precinct I read all of Frisco's notes and his timeline board. Mr. Weizner was with me during his wine tasting party where Andrew was murdered. "Frisco, can you think back to some of the other people who attended the party? Who was missing from the staff?"

"I have a list of all of the people who were present in the blue folder. Let's go through it together. Maybe I have it wrong, or perhaps we can come up with staff who weren't there."

"Let's go to my house for lunch."

"Great idea. I think better on a full stomach," Frisco replied. "And dessert."

"Okay."

We made our way back to my house and food.

"I don't see the supervisor or José or Charlotte's name on the list. The cook was there, passing out the appetizers. I saw Andrew briefly, but then, of course, he went missing, and Todd wasn't there. Then again, I don't think one of Dave's employees would have been invited."

"Can you get the budget sheet out? Something is missing. Something important but I just can't put my finger on it."

"There's large monthly payouts for oak barrels. Who does Hans buy his barrels from?" Frisco asked.

"He doesn't, why?"

"It doesn't say that here." Frisco pointed to the ledger. "It states that Hans buys oak barrels locally from R&R Company."

"I've never heard of them."

"For good reason. The address is bogus. It's a vacant lot."

"So whose pocket was that money going into?"

"Do you have Charlotte's bank statements?"

{ 59 }

"He said that few people had intellectual resources sufficient to forego the pleasures of wine.
They could not otherwise contrive how to fill the interval between dinner and supper."
SAMUEL JOHNSON

I got dressed quickly and drove to meet with Mr. Weizner and his lawyer because Frisco said he wanted to speak to us.

At the sheriff's station, Mr. Weizner sat with his lawyer in the interrogation room. He looked up humbly at us. There was no smirking, no smart remarks. He looked like a man who had been beaten severely and lost and was ready to talk.

"My client has accepted a deal on the table that he would not be convicted of counterfeiting crimes and would like to make a statement," Mr. Rogers said.

"I think I've been framed for something I didn't do. Sure, I conned many people out of a lot of money. I blackmailed Dave when I found out he was stealing my bottles of wine, but I didn't murder anyone. Check the books. Charlotte kept the records, paid the bills."

"What do you mean you've been framed?" Frisco asked. "You're saying you didn't kill anyone but freely admit to stealing and counterfeiting wine. Someone hates you enough to go through all of this?" Frisco asked in disbelief. "Who hates you, Mr. Weizner?"

I could think of so many people who had been hurt by Hans.

"I'm guilty of many things, I freely admit that. I'm a fraud, I can be cruel, and I was angry with you, Daisy. I wanted you. I didn't want you to side with farm workers, and I didn't want you with Frisco. Clearly many people would like to see me go down but murder? I wouldn't kill."

Mr. Weizner was right. Someone set him up. My cell phone was ringing. "Hi, Charlotte. Is everything okay?" I asked.

"I didn't see you this morning so I'm checking in to make sure you're okay and see if Hans is behind bars for good. The paper didn't give out any information."

"I don't think he did it, Charlotte. Neither does Frisco."

"Of course, he did. Don't let him get off."

Why was Charlotte so interested? Who had the intelligence to frame Mr. Weizner?

"Oh, God, no," I whispered.

Frisco looked over at me. When I'd spoken with Charlotte about the books when she'd still been with Hans, I'd seen a checkbook laid out with entries for R&R Company.

No, not Charlotte. She wouldn't kill Todd; she loved him. They'd been engaged. Why would she kill him? "No worries, Charlotte. He's still in jail."

"Good, I would hate to see a murderer and thief get off, but Frisco's good at his job."

"Right. He is good at his job. I'll see you later this afternoon."

I was squeezing my phone tight after the exchange. Frisco pried it out of my hand.

"What was that all about?" Frisco asked when I ended the call.

"What if Charlotte set up Mr. Weizner? You made the case, you had the timeline, and you had a motive, but what if we haven't been looking at the right person?"

Frisco stood up. "What makes you say this? The only thing we found was a company that we couldn't account for. What's different?"

"I remembered that Charlotte, even if her books were right in payouts, had a second set of books. Why?"

"One thing I'm sure of is that Charlotte's smart, but I don't know if she and Hans are partners in all of this," Frisco replied.

{ 60 }

"Good wine ruins the purse;
bad wine ruins the stomach."
SPANISH SAYING

Frisco and I jumped into his truck and followed the police cars heading for my villa where Charlotte was working. "You really believe it's true? You really think Charlotte killed Todd?" I asked.

"Think about it. Todd and Charlotte were at the dinner party given by Andrew and his wife. Andrew told everyone there how he and Hans had stolen the wine and relabeled the bottles. Things went south when Todd dumped Charlotte for Katie. She had to get rid of Andrew and Todd to keep the scheme going, and because Todd was leaving her, Andrew and Dave stopped paying her. I think Dave may have put it all together and confronted her about the murders."

We pulled into the driveway of the villa. Frisco was out the door and into the tasting room before me. Charlotte was sitting behind her desk, waiting for our arrival it seemed.

"So you finally figured it out?" she said, pulling a gun out from under the desk.

"Put it down, Charlotte; it doesn't have to go down like this," Frisco said calmly.

"Oh, Frisco, yes, it does. I loved Todd, but he was stupid. I'm the one who devised the plan to rip off Hans. Todd got greedy and was going to cut me out of the money and leave me for Katie. Todd had to die."

"Why Dave, Charlotte?"

"He knew I'd killed Todd."

"How?" I asked.

"He saw me kill him. Dave was meeting with Hans to tell him that I'd killed Todd. I'm good friends with Timothy and went back into the kitchen where I placed the poison on Dave's plate; then I took the evidence and put it into Hans's safe. I was his assistant."

She looked at me in a crazy way. "There is just far too much brutality in this world, don't you think, Daisy? Even your little friend Katie got in the way. She was trying to take Todd away from me. Couldn't keep her nose out of my business."

This is all too crazy. Poor Katie, she didn't deserve to be mixed up in this.

"It was me, all me. I killed Andrew, and I killed Todd and Katie for stealing and cheating on me. I killed and framed Dave. It was all me." Charlotte was laughing hysterically. Then she pointed the gun at herself and fired. The gun exploded, and she fell back onto the floor. Frisco tried to stop her. He rushed over, but it was too late.

"What have you done, Charlotte?" I screamed.

Frisco pulled the gun out of her hand. I didn't want her to die like this. I gathered myself together and walked out of the room, squeezing past Frisco.

{ 61 }

"The best use of bad wine is
to drive away poor relations."
FRENCH PROVERB

The following week my life was getting back on track. Tonight was a big night for me — The Grey Stallion's wine-tasting party. Getting dressed upstairs, I ran to the bathroom to look at my hair and the new dress I had purchased. The door slowly opened. It was Mike. He had a gun in his hand.

"It's been a long time, Daisy."

I took a step back from the door. "I'm sorry, Mike. I was a stupid kid. I helped my mom. I thought you were dead."

"You buried me. Your mom told me. It's one of the last things she said. Now it's your turn."

He grabbed my hair and dragged me to my bedroom.

"Let go of me, Mike! I'm sorry. I thought you were dead. I loved my mom. Why are you doing this?" I screamed.

"It's payback, Daisy, and I want one more thing from you."

I heard Freeway barking frantically. "Get off of me! You're alive for God's sake. Get out of here."

He lifted my dress. I squeezed my legs tightly together and fought him, pushing myself away. He held me roughly while I screamed at the top of my lungs.

"You're going to enjoy it, Daisy. Just one last moment together."

I kicked him in the groin, then crawled to the door. From the corner of my eye, I saw him lift his gun.

Suddenly Mike flew away from me. His gun dropped to the ground. I crawled over to it. Frisco had him by the neck and was strangling him. He slammed his fist into Mike's face. I heard the sickening sound of bones crunching. He didn't move.

"Call the police," he commanded.

I grabbed my cell off the bedside table and called the police. Thank God Frisco came early for the party. "Thank you," was all I could get out between sobs. I walked toward Frisco slowly. My legs felt like they were in cement. All I wanted was his arms around me.

Freeway came bounding into my room. "I think you need to thank your dog. She never barks like that so I knew something was wrong as soon as I heard her. She deserves a steak dinner."

I bent down and patted her head. "She shall have it." We'd been through a lot together. I smiled at Frisco and held Freeway tight.

"You okay?" Frisco asked worriedly.

"I am now."

The police handcuffed Mike. He glared at me with anger and defiance.

"It's not over, Daisy."

I didn't think it ever would be.

{ 62 }

"Wine is the most healthful
and most hygienic of beverages."
LOUIS PASTEUR

Frisco dropped by the next morning bearing gifts of croissants, peach jam, and champagne. A perfect combination for my frayed nerves.

"What did you do about the party?"

Jack stood at the front gates and waved people off. With all the police, sirens, and flashing lights there was not a lot for me to do. "I'll talk to the reporters, and later we'll do a grand opening of our winery."

"What about us?" I looked up at him shyly.

"I plan on having you around for the rest of my life."

"I can't think of anywhere I'd rather be than in your life and right now in your arms."

Frisco came to me, and I wrapped myself around his neck. I never wanted this moment to end.

About the Author

L. Lee Kane is the author of *The Black Madonna* and *Chilled to the Bones*. Her books have translated into forty-two languages in forty countries. A school psychologist who has traveled extensively, she lives in the Central Valley of California. She is currently at work on her next novel.

Visit her at www.lindaleekane.com.

www.ingramcontent.com/pod-product-compliance
Lightning Source LLC
Chambersburg PA
CBHW021222260626
47172CB00002B/559